RAISED IN CAPTIVITY

Also by CHUCK KLOSTERMAN

Fiction

Downtown Owl

The Visible Man

Nonfiction

Fargo Rock City:
A Heavy Metal Odyssey in Rural North Dakota

Sex, Drugs, and Cocoa Puffs:
A Low Culture Manifesto

Killing Yourself to Live:
85% of a True Story

Chuck Klosterman IV:
A Decade of Curious People and Dangerous Ideas

Eating the Dinosaur

I Wear the Black Hat:
Grappling with Villains (Real and Imagined)

But What If We're Wrong?
Thinking About the Present As If It Were the Past

Chuck Klosterman X:
A Highly Specific, Defiantly Incomplete History
of the Early 21st Century

Penguin Press   New York   2019

RAISED IN CAPTIVITY

CHUCK KLOSTERMAN

Fictional Nonfiction

PENGUIN PRESS
An imprint of Penguin Random House LLC
penguinrandomhouse.com

Library of Congress Cataloging-in-Publication Data

Names: Klosterman, Chuck, 1972- author.
Title: Raised in captivity : fictional nonfiction / Chuck Klosterman.
Description: New York : Penguin Press, 2019
Identifiers: LCCN 2018038237 (print) | LCCN 2018047295 (ebook) |
    ISBN 9780735217942 (ebook) | ISBN 9780735217928 (hardcover)
Classification: LCC PS3611.L67 (ebook) | LCC PS3611.L67 A6 2019 (print) |
    DDC 813/.6--dc23
LC record available at https://lccn.loc.gov/2018038237

Printed in the United States of America
10 9 8 7 6 5 4 3 2 1

Designed by Daniel Lagin

Contents

RAISED IN CAPTIVITY

Raised in Captivity

IT WAS BETTER THAN ANTICIPATED, AT LEAST FOR THE FIRST TWENTY minutes. Not $1,200 better, because that's impossible. But still: Hot towels for the jowls. Enough territory to extend your entire left leg into the aisle without fear of sanction or reprisal. A glass of orange juice while still at the gate, served in a glass made of glass. He thought to himself, "I could get used to this." But that thought was a lie. He would never get used to this, even if it became the only way he traveled anywhere. The experience would never seem unremarkable. It would always feel gratuitous in the best possible way.

Would he read a novel or watch a movie? Maybe neither. The chair was so supple, perhaps he'd just sit there and stare robotically ahead, fixated on the degree to which he wasn't uncomfortable. There was Wi-Fi in the cabin. Maybe he'd send a group email to all his old high school chums, playfully bragging about the altitude from which the message had been sent. His friends didn't understand his job, but they would understand that. He couldn't tell them what his salary was, but he could show them how his company treated its employees. That might scan as pompous, of course. It might make him seem like a bit of a douche, and he didn't aspire to become the kind of person he'd always been conditioned to hate. But he was proud of himself, maybe for the first time. His life had changed, and this was proof.

He asked the attendant about the flight's duration. She estimated just over three hours. He got up to use the lavatory, delighted by the absence of a line. He wondered if it would be different from the restrooms in coach—larger, perhaps, or cleaner. And it was. It was slightly larger and slightly cleaner. But he barely noticed those details, because it also included a puma.

He immediately closed the door and returned to his seat.

For a solid seventy seconds, he considered doing nothing at all. "Don't panic. Don't choke. There's no way what you think you saw could possibly be the thing that it is." He reached down into his leather satchel and felt around for his book. His father had once told him that the key to life was an ability to ignore other people's imaginary problems. But he wasn't sure to whom this particular problem belonged, or if it was real or imaginary, or if his father had ever considered what that advice actually implied.

He again got up from his seat and walked to the lavatory. He cracked the door two inches ajar, enough for the automatic light to illuminate. He peered into the tiny room. There it was, sitting on the lid of the toilet, looking back with an empty intensity that matched his own.

He closed the door and returned to his seat.

Seeing the puma a second time did not prompt the internal reaction he'd anticipated. He was, for whatever reason, a bit ambivalent. On the one hand, he was trapped in a contained space with a two-hundred-pound cat. On the other hand, at least the puma was truly there. If the lavatory had been empty, it would have meant he was hallucinating. Better to be a noncrazy person in peril than a crazy person who was safe. He turned to the passenger sitting to his immediate right, an older man in a pin-striped suit who was drinking his second martini.

"Excuse me," he said to the gentleman in 2D. "This is going to sound bizarre, but . . . have you used the restroom on this flight?"

"No," said the man. "Why do you ask?"

"I don't know how to explain this," he began, almost murmuring. "I don't even know how this happened, or what this means, or what you're supposed to do with the information I'm about to give you. Part of me thinks I shouldn't even tell you this, although I don't know why I would think that, since I'm sure this is something you'll want to know. None of this makes sense. None of it. But I just got up and went to the lavatory, twice. And both times, when I opened the door, there was a puma in the bathroom."

"A puma?"

"Yes. I realize how insane that must sound. I'm sorry."

"A puma? In the bathroom?"

"Yes."

"A cougar."

"Yes."

"A mountain lion."

"Yes. Sure. A mountain lion."

"A catamount."

"What? I don't know. Maybe. Yes?"

The older man in the pinstriped suit leaned across 2C, dipping his head into the aisle. His hair smelled like rubbing alcohol and coconut water. He studied the closed restroom door. It looked like a door. He resituated himself back in his chair, straightened his jacket by the lapels, and took a quick sip of his translucent beverage. His hands and feet were massive, too big for his frame.

"Let me ask you something," the older man said. "And don't take this the wrong way. I'm not being judgmental. I'm drinking gin in the middle of the morning. I'm no priest. And you don't seem like a kid on drugs. But tell me if you're on drugs. We just left California. I get it."

"I'm not on drugs," he replied.

"Not even the prescription variety? Lexapro? Valium?"

"No. Nothing."

"Any history of mental illness? Again, no offense intended."

"No, and I'm not offended."

The two men looked into each other's eyes, hunching their shoulders and leaning closer. The interaction adopted a conspiratorial tone. They spoke in stage whispers. The other passengers barely noticed and didn't care.

"Tell me this," said the older man. "What are your theories?"

"My theories?"

"In terms of how this could have happened."

"I have no idea," the younger man said. "I have no theories."

"Try," said the older man. "We're just brainstorming. There are no wrong answers."

This was not what the younger man had expected to hear. But he had no expectations at all, so it wasn't awkward or off-putting. He did what he was told.

"I suppose it's possible that some millionaire might own a puma as an exotic pet, and he was hauling it across the country, and it escaped from its cage in the cargo hold and crawled through the air-conditioning vents, and it somehow ended up in the bathroom."

"Excellent," said the older man. "Let's have another."

"I don't know. Maybe it prowled down from the Hollywood Hills and ended up at LAX, and it was drawn into the airplane hangar by the warmth of the cooling jet engines, but it got scared when the engines were restarted and scampered into the only cavelike crevice it could find, which was the restroom inside the aircraft."

"Less plausible," said the older man. "But still possible. Keep going."

"Maybe this is a psychological experiment, and the puma is a trained puma, and I'm being watched. Maybe this is some kind of radical research project. And maybe you're the scientist who came up with the experiment, which is why you're seated next to me and asking these questions."

"That's compelling," said the older man. "But let me assure you—if this is a research project, I'm not part of it."

"Maybe this is advertising. Maybe this is some kind of guerilla marketing for Puma basketball shoes."

"Too high-concept. Try again."

"Maybe this is a symptom of some deeper problem," the younger person continued, oddly delighted by the older person's interest in his improvisational hypotheses. "Maybe mankind has encroached upon nature too much, to the point of no return. Maybe animals and humans will start coming into conflict all the time, and this is the beginning of that looming crisis. Maybe in five or ten years, it will not be uncommon to encounter a puma on an airplane."

"Intriguing," said the older man. "But let's not lose focus on the moment. Keep yourself grounded."

"The puma could be rabid," the younger man speculated. "Rabid animals lose their instinctual fear of humans. It might have just slinked onto the plane in a state of confusion, camouflaged by the carpet. I mean, look at the carpet. The carpet is taupe. Taupe is pure puma. Or maybe he's some type of hypermodern service animal. Maybe instead of getting a seeing-eye dog, you can now get a seeing-eye puma. It's also possible the TSA has started using pumas to sniff for narcotics, or maybe for bombs. Who knows? Maybe pumas are better at bomb detection than beagles."

"Pumas have a relatively weak sense of smell," said the older man. "But these are viable theories."

"I suppose a deranged person could have done this intentionally," the younger man said, abruptly alarmed by the prospect that he'd stumbled upon the true explanation. "A terrorist. If the intention of a terrorist is to incite terror, what would be more terrifying than being attacked by a puma on an airplane? It would change air travel forever. Who would bring an infant on a flight if there were any possibility of a puma encounter? Who would let their elderly mother travel alone? There are so many ways this could be done. It wouldn't be difficult. You heavily sedate the puma and place it in a canvas bag. You place the bag on the outskirts of the airport and you bribe a baggage handler. The handler hauls the bag planeside and a passenger with a fake passport casually picks it up, claiming it's hockey equipment or medical supplies or the fossilized remains of a saber-toothed cat. The passenger gets the bag on board and dumps it in the restroom, unzipped. The puma rouses itself. I realize pumas aren't normally aggressive, but this puma is hungry, and bewildered, and trapped in a small space. He's weaponized. Some entitled businessman with a bloated bladder opens the bathroom door. The puma pounces."

Their noses were now six inches apart. The old man raised his eyebrows. The younger man tried to construct an expression of concern, but he felt himself smirking. His puma theories were above average.

"Will you be having lunch?" a female voice intoned from behind the younger man's skull. "We have a cheese lasagna with a side salad and we have sliced chicken breast with wild ramps." The men broke eye contact and bolted up in their seats. The younger man ordered the lasagna. The older man said he only wanted another martini. They both relaxed as the stewardess moved on to the third row and repeated the same information to the woman in 3A. She ordered the lasagna as well. The man in 3B went with the chicken. When the orders were complete, they could hear the woman in 3A ask the man in 3B if he could let her pass, as she needed to use the restroom.

"Here we go," said the old man in the pinstriped suit. He turned away, toward the window.

"Shouldn't I tell her about the puma?" asked the younger man.

"That's not my problem. Or yours," said the older man, still looking away. "We're all in this together."

Execute Again

Exègèse Again

THIS IS THE TENTH INTERVIEW I'VE GRANTED SINCE THE ELECTION. At this point, I feel like the backstory has been more than sufficiently covered. I thought the gal from *The New York Times Magazine* did an especially comprehensive job, despite getting a few key details incorrect. All of this has been addressed elsewhere, arguably to the point of overkill. That said, I do understand why certain people are enamored with my story. They think it explains so much. They think it reflects something that can't be otherwise seen. Is that true? I suppose if people think that it does, it does. And I certainly don't mind talking about my life, since my life is my life.

I'm not going to rehash the biographical details. Those are easy enough to find on the Internet. I also won't respond to statements made by any of my peers. They have the right to think or believe whatever they want. I'll only tell you what I remember firsthand: He showed up in August, just before my junior year. There was no fanfare. It wasn't like anybody announced, "Here's Jasper Lovelace, the wonderful new football coach. He's going to change everything about reality." Remember, this was a town so small that it wasn't even included on most Oklahoma road maps. There wasn't a single stoplight. There was no newspaper. There was no news. We all just show up for the first day of football practice, and Lovelace is the man waiting in the equipment room. Mirrored sunglasses. Massive beard, massive gut. Clothes from Target or Kmart. Some kids thought he seemed gay, but I'd have never made that inference on my own.

None of this was a big deal to anyone. Nobody cared about football at my school. I didn't care and I was on the damn team. The coach was just the coach. But I must say—this guy, this person, was immediately goofy. Immediately. For the first four days, we never touch a football. We don't even go outside. Lovelace sits us in the school cafeteria and meticulously lectures about subjects that appear to have no application to anything related to sports. Clocks. He spends the first two hours explaining how clocks work, from a mechanical standpoint. He talks about how the ocean is 95 percent unexplored. He talks about math without using numbers. The Civil War. The Crucifixion. Chopping wood. Kierkegaard's "philosophy of repetition," which I'd totally forgotten about until I saw it mentioned in his obituary. There are some parables and some fairy tales and a few extremely long jokes without punch lines. It's disjointed. It's granular. But the big takeaway from these four interminable days is that our football team is only going to run one play, for the entire season. He mentions this, almost in passing, six or seven times. We do not take these words at face value. Why would we? What does that even mean, you know?

On the fifth day, a Friday, we finally go outside. It's raining like crazy. Lots of lightning, scary thunder. For a few minutes it hails, and we all wonder if maybe the firehouse will blow the tornado siren. But we stay out there. For the first hour, all we do is conditioning drills. These are like the conditioning drills Rocky Balboa did in that movie where he fights the Russian: We have to throw straw bales and run through the local swamp and shovel grain. It's more or less unpaid farmwork, and everybody wants to quit. Farmwork was what most of us had joined the team to avoid. But there's just something hypnotic about this fat guy with the dumb name and the dumb beard. He's so composed. So calm, so above it all. It's the first time any of us have ever encountered a coach who doesn't yell and never swears. He makes all his instructions seem self-evident. We eventually walk over to the practice field and start learning this one specific play—the play he halfway explained during his little speech about Kierkegaard. It's the most convoluted educational experience I've ever had, still to this day. An old classmate of mine is now a neurosurgeon, and he claims it was trickier than anything he experienced in med school. It took us a long time just to figure out how to line up in the correct formation. All eleven players—even the linemen—had to memorize all this intricate footwork, which I can only compare to learning how to foxtrot and moonwalk at the same time. Every blocker was pulling and crossing, and if any one person's timing was microscopically imperfect we'd all collide. How can I possibly explain this? It was like one of those Rube Goldberg machines: The quarterback takes the snap and hands it to a halfback breaking to his right. That halfback immediately hands the ball to the fullback going left, and then the fullback delivers it to a wingback curling toward the middle. These three handoffs all happen within a two-second window. When it works, it all happens so fast that it almost looks like nothing happened at all. From a helicopter, the motion of the play was supposed to resemble water spiraling down a drain. It seemed impossible to get this correct. I have no idea how many attempts it took before we got it even halfway right. Way more than a hundred. Maybe closer to a thousand. A handful of guys stopped coming to practice the

following Monday. Lovelace didn't care at all. He compared them to people who believe the moon landing was faked.

We work on this play constantly, over and over and over again. It's
usually all we do for the entire three-hour practice. For the first week or so,
we assume this must be some kind of Zen lesson, because Lovelace tried
to introduce us to Buddhism back in the cafeteria. We all assume we'll
eventually add the other offensive plays. The *real* plays. You know? But as
the days progress, it becomes clear that we're not adding anything. This
is the entire playbook. We don't even have a name for the play, because it
doesn't need a name. There's nothing to differentiate it from. We never
put in a punt formation, because we are told we'll never punt, ever, under
any circumstance. There will be no field goal attempts. There will be no
passing plays. The night before our first game, Lovelace draws up a defensive alignment on the locker-room chalkboard and lists which eleven
players will start and what specific positions they'll occupy. But we never
actually practice playing defense, based on his argument that it won't
matter. "This schematic is a projection of where you're supposed to stand
at the inception of your opponent's action," he said. That was how he
talked. "When presented with the opportunity, initiate contact with the
ball carrier." That was the extent of his defensive instruction.

Now, I realize some of this has been explained elsewhere, particularly in that unnecessarily contentious piece in *Jacobin*. But I will sum-
marize it again, since I know that's what you want and I know that's what
you're here for. Jasper Lovelace had no football experience whatsoever.
There was no mystery around that fact. He would straight-up say, "I am
not a football coach." I'm not sure what he was, to be honest, or what he
thought he was. He seemed a little like an engineer without an engineer-
ing degree. He liked to describe himself as an artist without creativity.
The one thing I do know is that he designed this singular play to mirror

the movement of wristwatch gears, which was the reason for all that horology shit back in the cafeteria. Lovelace's theory was that an offensive football team could generate a spiraling clockwise motion at the point of attack, and the sheer mass of the whirling players—including the defenders, who would be swept up against their will—would involuntarily propel the ball carrier forward and downward, into the turf but beyond the line of scrimmage. It was basically a physics equation. It did not matter what the opponent did, or even if they jammed the entire defensive squad onto the exact spot where they knew the ball was going. If executed correctly, the result was supposed to be the same, every time: The play would unspool, the mass of humanity would be untangled, and the wingback would always, *always*, end up 2.7 yards beyond the line of scrimmage, with a standard deviation of plus or minus four inches. Lovelace worked all this out on reams and reams of graph paper, which he later burned. But once the play was memorized and internalized, we didn't need any pictures or calculations. Once his worldview was established, the logic became unassailable: If we ran this play correctly four times in a row, we would gain exactly 10.8 yards, which would constitute a first down. We would then run it four more times, and—once again—gain exactly 10.8 yards, constituting another first down. We could theoretically do this for the whole game, theoretically scoring a theoretical touchdown on every theoretical possession. It was—theoretically—100 percent efficient. This is the reason Jasper Lovelace believed investing any time into a defensive strategy was irrelevant. If we stopped an opponent on just one possession, purely by accident, the war would be over. Because we would score every time and they would psychologically surrender.

The logistics, of course, were not that simple. We famously lost the season opener 88–0, and everybody in town thought Lovelace was an imbecile. Everyone was like, "What in the hell does this turkey tit think he's doing? This isn't football." But you know, it wasn't football, so that criticism didn't bother him. I've never seen a man care less about other people's opinions. Nothing changed. We kept practicing the same play, no matter how ridiculous it made us feel. There was never any talk of scouting the opposition or giving 110 percent or considering what any of this was supposed to signify. There was never any deeper message. We'd just execute the play in practice and Lovelace would say, "Execute again." No emotion, no intensity. Just, "Execute again." So we'd run it again. No huddles, no introspection. We lost the second game 54–0. It was humiliating, but Lovelace harbored no shame. "Execute again." I found myself wanting to be more like him. I started wearing mirrored sunglasses. We lost the third game 27–0. "Execute again. Execute again." We lost the fourth game 18–12, on the road, eliminating us from playoff contention before the season was even half finished. We were a laughingstock. You could actually hear people laughing in the stands. But on the bus ride home, after we scored those first twelve points, Lovelace cryptically looks back from the front seat of the bus and says, "It's happening." None of us will ever forget the way he said that. I can still hear his voice, right now, today. It haunts me. I have no idea why we stuck with him. I guess it seemed like we were inventing something other people couldn't understand. It was a little like a cult. It *was* a cult, probably. So we play the fifth game, and we win. We win 32–28. And then the following week, we win 66–20. People think it's cute that this is happening. They think it's charming that a football team can win a game with only one play. We're on the local news in Stillwater. The next week is homecoming, and the final score is 72–14. No one can touch us. We finish the season 6–4, winning our last game 112–0. Our wingback, Ricky Milner, breaks every scoring record in the state. But of course no college recruits him, because he never has a single carry that goes for more than three yards. By the end of the year, everyone in town is talking about how Jasper Lovelace is a genius and how we'll undoubtedly go undefeated next season and win state.

The rest of the story is the stuff everyone already knows. Lovelace inexplicably resigns that December and goes on to become the person he eventually became. Missing his funeral will bother me forever. Ricky Milner is now Richard Milner, who of course is our president-elect. We lost touch, Ricky and I, but I'm so proud to have known him, all those years ago. Who would ever have believed that the kid who used to shotgun Old Milwaukee in my basement would somehow become president of the United States? The boy who was our quarterback went on to design the first artificial lung from organic fibers. Our old left tackle is arguably the finest living architect in North America, having just designed that astonishing library in Vancouver. I assume you've read T. R. Henke's novel, where the titular character is unambiguously named "Lovey Jasper." Henke played halfback. I don't remember him reading a single book all through high school, but now they say he's probably going to win the Pulitzer. So wild. Every single person on that team ended up with an amazing life, which can't be a coincidence. We were taught things they don't teach anymore. We were taught things that were never taught, ever, to anyone else. Jasper Lovelace convinced us that we did not have to live like normal people. He rebuilt our brains. With the exception, I suppose, of my brain. I'm just a regular guy, which is why you're here now, talking to me about the new president and all those other boys who keep changing the world. I'm the lone contradiction, and the media uses that against me. But please let me say, once more, for the record: I did not do the things they say I did. I did not kill those people. I can't explain how their bone fragments got in my garage or why someone would have put them there. I don't even know 260 people. I mean, come on—260 unconnected murders? Am I a monster? Am I a machine? The trial was a farce. My lawyer deserves to be disbarred, and that judge was a narcissistic clown. But I will appeal. Believe me. I will appeal. I will be vindicated. I will not die for what I have not done.

Toxic Actuality

T HEY STROLLED THROUGH THE QUAD, THE ONLY PART OF CAMPUS
still resembling the institution that had hired them years before.
It was the sector of campus always photographed for brochures,
but only during October, latently suggesting that the whole geographic
region existed in a state of perpetual autumn. The leaves were always
floating to earth and a sweater was always enough. One man was sixty-
eight and the other was forty-five, so they were the same age.

"I'm not sure how I'm supposed to do this anymore," Benjamin said
for the third time that day. "I go to the dean of arts and sciences, exactly
at noon. I'm exactly on time. But the kid is already there, so I'm asked to
wait outside. The kid says he won't speak if I'm in the room. About twenty
minutes later, the door opens and the kid leaves. Doesn't say anything to
me. Doesn't look at me. The dean calls me into his office, we talk for
maybe five minutes, and then I'm told to sign a document that validates
the student's complaint and states that I will accept his perspective on
microaggressions."

"Will there be repercussions?" Geoffrey asked. "Could you be fired?"

"I don't think I'll be fired," said Benjamin. "Maybe if it happens again, or if it keeps happening. I mean, it could easily happen again, either with him or with someone else."

"What was the nature of the dispute? You never really explained." Geoffrey was treading lightly.

"I have no idea," said Benjamin. "I'm teaching the text. The student says the text is racist. I say, 'No, the text is *about* racism.' The student concedes that this might have been the author's intent but that the language itself is racist, because the author didn't recognize his privilege. The other white students agree. The whole class is white. I think, 'Great, this will be a real discussion.' But they don't want a discussion. They only want me to admit that the text is racist. So again, I say it's *about* racism, which is the reason we're reading it. The same student tells me I couldn't possibly understand, because my identity has never been oppressed. I tell him two of my grandparents died in the Holocaust. He asks if that means I support state-sponsored terrorism against Palestine. I tell him that his question is insane. Now, maybe I say *insane* louder than necessary. I'm sure I did. But still. So then he tells me it's misogynistic to refer to him as crazy. He says that specific word is a form of oppression. I tell him that I never used the specific word *crazy* and—even if I had—it couldn't be misogynistic, because he isn't female. He starts inserting the word *intersectionality* into non-sequitur sentences, and I kind of laugh. I realize I shouldn't have laughed, but I did. He then marches out of the room. Six other students follow him. And then, two days later, the dean sends me an email and says we need to meet, because I've been accused of humiliating a student and creating an unsafe environment. I truly don't know how I'm supposed to do this anymore."

Geoffrey, having heard this type of talk from Benjamin many times before, tried to swing the discussion toward abstraction. "You need to remember what things were like when you were in school. This happened in the early nineties, too. It happens every twenty or thirty years."

"No. You're wrong," Benjamin replied, shaking his fingers at no one in particular. "With all due respect, you're wrong about this. It's not the same. That was about people who didn't believe Anita Hill's testimony. That was about the ethics of listening to 2 Live Crew and Body Count. This is about how kids are being raised. They expect to live a life without intellectual conflict. They don't believe other ideas should even exist. I mean, come on. I didn't humiliate that kid. I didn't even yell at him. I said one word, maybe ten decibels higher than my previous sentence."

"Decibels increase exponentially," said Geoffrey. "A ten-decibel increase would actually be twice as loud."

"I think you're missing the point on purpose, Geoff."

"Then explain the point, Ben."

They were now using direct address, which meant the conversation was no longer amicable.

"The point," Benjamin said, "is that we're allowing these kids to live in a false reality. Which would be fine, except that we're also supposed to act like their false reality is rational. We're somehow allowing them to be fascist and childish at the same time. They won't be prepared for life. Take the kid I allegedly humiliated. What's going to happen the first time he has to confront an idea that contradicts his worldview? What's going to happen the first time his boss eviscerates him in front of his co-workers? How will he survive that? There's no way that kid will be able to handle the real world."

"But there is no real world," said Geoffrey. "That's what you don't understand."

"What?"

"There is no real world," said Geoffrey. "Or at least not a world any realer than this one."

They walked in silence for fifteen steps. They watched a squirrel disappear into a dead tree.

"Look," Geoffrey continued. "I know you think this place is some kind of sick incubator, and that the world outside is harsh and uncompromising, and that these kids are going to leave school fragile and deluded, and that they'll be dead on arrival. But that will never happen. The world you believe they're forcing upon us is the only world they will ever know. You think the kid who filed that complaint is going to graduate and become a construction worker? A nurse? A welder? That doesn't happen to the kids who go here, unless they want to write a memoir about it. Maybe they'll end up doing nothing, but they'll still be fine. They'll pretend to be broke until their parents die, and then they'll be as rich as their parents. This is the real world, for them and for us. Right here. Where we are, right now. This path they photograph for the brochure. This is it. This is the world."

They stopped walking to watch another squirrel. The rodent watched them back, nervous and bored.

"I don't accept that," Benjamin finally said. "That's illogical. That's like giving up."

"It's not up for your approval," replied Geoffrey. "It's not a motion that requires ratification. Quit talking about rationality. That's not part of this. That's never part of this. They're building their version of society, and we can either pretend we like it or find a different one. You and I did the same thing. People used to call me names I hated, pretty much whenever they felt like it. They would say those things to my face, and there was nothing I could do. So I chose to live my life in a place where that never happened. I chose a life where people don't talk like that, or at least not when I'm in the room. I'm sure some people still talk like that, somewhere out there, in places I'll never go. I'm sure a few people out there still talk the way *everyone* used to talk. But I haven't met a person like that in thirty years, and that is by design."

"That's not the same thing," said Benjamin.

"Nothing is the same," said Geoffrey. "Analogies don't work. Analogies only work on standardized tests, which is why we pretend they qualify as arguments. Things that seem the same are still different. When I was twenty, I had a summer job at a bakery. My boss yelled at me constantly, for being lazy. I didn't think I was lazy, but he did. Compared to him, maybe I was. But that's all over. These kids will never get yelled at for being lazy. That won't be part of their existence. They will only get yelled at when the kids who come after them decide they're holding antiquated beliefs about how the world is supposed to work, and that all the big ideas they once considered progressive are actually reactionary. So you're right. It's not the same. But what's the difference? There's still yelling."

They continued along the gravel lane another twenty yards, or maybe it was 18.3 meters. The path warped into a roundabout. There were four options in front of them: veer left (toward the part of campus that resembled an industrial park), veer right (toward the part of campus that resembled a hobo village), turn back (where they'd started from originally), or continue forward (out through the wrought-iron gates and into the ugly little town).

"So I'm just supposed to let this happen," Benjamin said, staring at the gate. "I'm just supposed to let some kid accuse me of things that aren't true, because he gets to decide what's real, because he's young and I'm not. Is that how it works now?"

"Yes," said Geoffrey. "That's how it works now, and that's how it has always worked. You need to get over this." And that was the end of the walk.

How Can This
Be the Place?

I HAVE THE KIND OF JOB WHERE I TAKE A SHOWER AT NIGHT, AFTER I GET home. When I was young, I always assumed I'd have a different kind of job, the kind of job where you take a shower in the morning, before you leave. That's not how things worked out. I went to college for three semesters, until I was broke. They told me to apply for a Pell Grant, but the application was more complicated than any of my classes. I needed to work for a while before I went back, and the only way to make real money was to take a job where you took a shower at night. I figured ten or twelve months of night showers would lead to a lifetime of morning showers, which is what I wanted. But you know, I also wanted a Honda Hurricane. Then I had to get my wisdom teeth pulled. Then my friends who were still enrolled at school convinced me to go to South Padre Island for a week and we all took turns driving, except I got a DUI in North Texas and had to wire some lawyer three grand to knock it down to reckless driving and minor in consumption. That was sixteen years ago. I've had a lot of different jobs in the interim, but my showering schedule has remained unchanged.

Some days are bad and some days are good. We all go to the bar after work on Thursdays, Fridays, and Mondays during football season. Those are the good days. The name of the place is Wing Bar, for reasons that are not exactly surprising. I like it, but I don't love it, for reasons that are not exactly surprising. The biggest upside is that I can leave my car overnight in the parking lot across the frontage road, if and when that becomes necessary. Wing Bar is a brick building with dark windows and a neon sign that only says WING BA. If you don't know what it is, you don't know what it is. That's the second-biggest upside. Last Thursday, as I crossed the four-lane street after parking my car, I saw a jittery man standing outside the bar, peering into the windows through cupped hands and constantly reexamining a front door that provided no numeric information. He was wearing a suit and a tie. That was odd. He kept looking at his phone and scrutinizing arbitrary architectural details surrounding the building. His thoughts were easy to read: "Is this the place? This must be the place. But how can this be the place?" It was like his brain was generating subtitles. I stop my approach and watch him worry, for no real reason. He makes a phone call. It lasts ten seconds and he nods for the duration. Then he turns away from the Wing Bar door and walks up the street, and I follow him, for no real reason.

I know where he's going before he does. He's going to P. D. Black's, the only other bar within walking distance. Black's is the nice bar. It's so nice that some people call it a tavern. It's so nice that, during the day, it feels like a restaurant. It's bright inside, and there's only one TV. They enforce the smoking ban. The bathroom stalls go all the way to the floor. I've been there maybe three times, always on a date.

The nervous man in the suit walks fast. He doesn't notice me, or anything else. When I finally push through the door of P. D. Black's he's already joined his group. It's three other men, all of them short, all of them white, all of them in suits. The other three suits appear to be teasing him for going to the wrong place. They drink thick brown liquor on ice.

The bar itself is oak and clean and shaped like a horseshoe, so I sit on the opposite end, twenty-five feet away. I order a pint of Killian's Red and watch them talk.

Part of me is worried that I'm too dirty to be in here, but that feeling passes. No one is looking at me. It's loud, and the assorted conversations drown out the music. Wing Bar is equally loud, but almost always in the opposite way. There are many attractive women here, or at least some attractive women, or at least women. They all seem to be wearing pencil skirts, which I love. I never knew pencil skirts were called "pencil skirts" until recently, when my nineteen-year-old niece explained that this is how one is supposed to refer to skirts of this style. I'd always thought they were just called small skirts. This, I suspect, is the kind of thing people learn in college. Not the only thing, obviously. But maybe it's an extra thing you learn, in an ancillary fashion, while you're primarily learning about accounting or hotel management or chemistry. It's a useless thing for a man to know, ninety-nine percent of the time. But then pencil skirts randomly come up in conversation, and either you know what they are or you don't. I've had to educate myself.

Beer is expensive in a place like this, but who cares. I'm not destitute. I drink seven. Watching these short guys in suits is awkwardly mesmerizing, despite the fact that their banter is only audible when they all laugh. It looks like they're constantly arguing, but no one ever gets mad. They drink slowly. They drink like people who intend to drive home. For the first hour, I try to make myself annoyed by their presence. I want to dislike them. But I don't. I can't. It's useless to get angry over strangers. If we concede that life is not fair, we must also concede that it has to be unfair to someone else's benefit. There's no way around that. Maybe they deserve it, maybe they don't. Maybe no one deserves anything. Maybe being smart enough to have a job where you wear a suit isn't worth the various trade-offs, such as being too dumb to realize how lame this bar is. By the time I start my eighth Killian's, the only sensation I feel is curiosity. Not about them, so much, but about myself. I'm drunk enough to climb inside my most vulnerable thoughts. I pick up my beer and walk over to their table. Why not? It's a free country.

"Excuse me," I say. They all freeze. They're robots. "Can I ask you a question?"

The four suits take turns looking at each other, unable to mask their confusion. One of them says okay, and then they all say okay. I think they might be drunker than me, despite having consumed half as much alcohol.

I pose my query to the table: "What have you guys been talking about?"

Again, they haphazardly glance at each other instead of looking back at me. The silence lasts longer than it should. These are bad robots.

"Bro," says the nervous man I followed three hours earlier. "We weren't talking about you. I swear to God. We weren't talking about anybody."

I had forgotten where I was and how I was dressed, and that my hands are covered in scars.

"Oh, no," I say. "No no no. I'm not that kind of person. No way. Never. I don't want trouble. I'm not making accusations. I'm just legitimately curious about what you've been talking about tonight."

They all relax, instantly. A little too much, the way only drunk people can relax.

"That's my only question," I reiterate. "What have you boys been discussing?"

"Gary's wife's vagina," says one, and two of them laugh like orangutans on nitrous.

"No, seriously," I say, turning to the non-laughing man I assume to be Gary.

"Why do you possibly care?"

"It's not that I care," I say. "I just want to know. For my own purposes."

The four suits can't seem to accept the simplicity of my request. They smile and squint and stammer. The guy who made the vagina joke finally tries to explain. He's terrible at explaining things.

"I don't think we've been talking about anything," he claims. "We work together, so we've been talking about work, but work sucks, so not really. We're all in a fantasy baseball league, so we talked about which guys still get steals and which guys still get saves. Gary has a little kid. We talked about the kid. The National are playing here next month, but none of us can go, so we talked about how we're not going to see the National. How's that? Is that what you need?"

"But you've been sitting here for three hours," I say. "There must be more. Didn't you talk about books or movies or anything else?"

"Books? I don't think we've ever talked about books. I guess we did talk about the last *Star Wars* movie. We all hate it."

"I don't mean movies like *Star Wars*."

"You don't like *Star Wars*?"

"No, that's not what I mean. It's just that I thought you'd be talking about different kinds of movies, or current events, or maybe tennis."

"Why would we be talking about tennis?"

"I don't know," I said, and I didn't. "You say you all work in the same office?"

"He and I met in law school," said the vagina-joke maker, pointing toward Probable Gary, "and then we both got jobs at their firm," dismissively waving the back of his hand at the other two robots.

"You're lawyers."

"Yeah," he replied. "We're lawyers."

"That's funny," I said, even though it wasn't. "You know, I needed a lawyer once. I committed a crime in another state, by accident. Kind of a bad crime, and I didn't know what I was supposed to do. I thought it might ruin my life. But I ended up talking to some lawyer over the telephone, and we had two or three short conversations, and he said he could fix everything for around three thousand dollars. And he did! I ended up getting charged with a couple of not-so-bad crimes and I never even had to go back for the court date. I still don't know how that worked. I never even met the lawyer in person."

"Was it a felony?"

"I don't even know. It was a DUI."

"Oh, sure," said the vagina-joke maker. "You can do that. That's not hard. It's harder than it used to be, but still not difficult."

"I had no idea," I said. "It seemed so crazy at the time."

"It is crazy," said the nervous little man I'd followed up the street. "That's the only thing you learn in law school that's useful: Laws are crazy on purpose. Everything is negotiable. If you make a law complicated enough, you can apply it any way you want. You just need to make sure it's so complicated that no normal person can understand it, unless they went to law school." He took a bird-sized sip of bourbon and continued. "What do you do? This doesn't seem like your kind of place."

"Lots of things," I say. "But right now, Sheetrock."

"I've heard of that," said Probable Gary.

We'd reached the point in the conversation where something had to change. Either they had to begrudgingly ask me to sit down or I had to make up an excuse to walk away. I take the latter option. There is nothing more to be gained from this. I carry my beer into the bathroom, enter a stall, close the door, and pour the remainder of the pint down my throat. I take a long piss and pay my bill. It's so high I need to use my debit card. The night air is still warm when I get outside, and more humid than earlier. No traffic on the street, in either direction. Why did I ask if they were talking about tennis? They must think I'm an idiot. I walk back toward my car, which I think I can still probably drive. I pass the Wing Bar and consider popping in. The other guys might still be in there. But then again, what would be the point? What would we do? Drink more drinks? Complain about *Star Wars*? Nobody deserves anything, everything is negotiable, and I need to take a shower.

The Truth
About Food

I T STARTED WITH A QUESTION FROM A SIX-YEAR-OLD, WHICH IS THE only way it could have happened at all. It was a question only a child would ask: "Do animals eat healthy?" A few of the scientists chuckled. Jokes were made, mostly for the benefit of the chaperones. But when the field trip was over and the kids had left the facility, a not-so-casual argument erupted in the lab.

"Of course they do," was the response from the senior researchers, followed by various versions of the phrase "How could they not?" The baseline contention was that nonhuman mammalian life pursues whatever their bodies need, devoid of choice or misplaced agency. The horse eats grain and hay because the horse is naturally compelled to do so. The lion eats a zebra because that is the lion's instinct. Humans are the only animals with the potential to want what they should not have, with the possible exception of domesticated dogs and cats (since those animals' lives are dictated by the flawed judgment of humans).

"But maybe not," replied the junior researchers, half in jest (but only half). "Isn't it possible that wild animals thrive *despite* their flawed diets?" The digestive systems of horses are able to break down the trace protein that exists in alfalfa, and the evolution of their horse teeth requires that they be herbivores. But is this really in their best interest? Would it potentially be good for a horse to eat another horse? Lions get zinc from zebra hearts and vitamin A from zebra livers, but are those limited options ideal? A lion has no access to sweet potatoes. Perhaps that's to the lion's detriment. Wild animals can only live in the way they understand, but that doesn't mean it's necessarily the best way possible.

The debate percolated among the lab workers for months, inevitably reduced to a core dispute over the character of ecology. The central issue was unscientific: Could the natural world be wrong? Is the natural world, by definition, the way the world is naturally supposed to be? For a handful of junior researchers, the possibility that it wasn't became a fixation that collapsed into obsession. Whatever they'd studied in the past was incrementally discarded, replaced by a desire to understand if the diet of feral animals was ideal or substandard. It was not a straightforward pursuit. You can't just start feeding bananas to jaguars. A musk ox won't eat salmon, even if you spice it with paprika. It seemed cruel to force animals to eat food they did not readily want, simply to see if it made them better or worse. Instead, the scientists pursued their quest through a back door. Instead of studying the consumer, they would focus on the consumed. They would study food itself—but not in the way it had been studied in the past. They would not look at food as nutritionists. They would look at food through the prism of biocentrism and panpsychism—in short, the belief that everything in the universe possesses some level of consciousness. This, as one might expect, was frowned upon by most of their more established peers. But this was an era when traditional science was trusted less, so radical concepts could be engaged. It was the style of the time.

Obviously, the data those researchers collected retroactively justifies the unconventionality of their approach. And (of course) that data still remains suppressed, for reasons that are equally easy to justify. But that doesn't mean the results aren't real. It only means they can't be discussed in public.

As one would expect, the full academic details are convoluted and tedious. We certainly won't outline them here. All that really matters is the upshot: As it turns out, it is consciousness that generates the material universe, not the other way around. Food is alive. It has a life force, just like all things that grow and multiply. All the qualities we long viewed as food's essential value—its vitamins, its minerals, its fiber—are worthless constructs. Calcium strengthens bones, but just barely. Vitamin K helps with blood coagulation, but not enough to stop anyone from bleeding to death. The difference between a handful of over-the-counter multivitamins and a handful of gravel is negligible. The myth of nutrition is not far removed from the myth of trolls causing disease. Most of what we eat has no purpose beyond rudimentary caloric fuel. Medically speaking, carrots and Kit Kats are identical. A Big Mac is transposable with tofu. What actually matters about food is more intangible. Food contains an existential power that cannot be measured or captured. It is, at risk of mixing metaphors, the juice of life. But (of course) no life force is eternal. The moment food stops living is the same moment its power begins to fade. This represents the massive advantage wild animals have over humans—the food they consume is almost always more alive. It's not what they eat, but how and when. The horse may prefer the flavor of oats, but his strength is sustained by uncut grass. The lion chomps the zebra while the zebra's heart still pumps, and that is what gives the lion a level of power no human can match. Even rotting carrion is closer to life than anything at Panera Bread.

When it comes to eating, humans are simply doing it wrong. Eat an apple while it still hangs on the tree and the life force is colossal. You share the vigor of the tree in totality, all the way down to its subterranean roots. But pluck that same apple off its branch and the power is immediately reduced by half. Twenty-four hours after harvest, the apple retains (maybe) 10 percent of its value; bake it into a pie and you're left with (maybe) .02 percent of the original magnetism. This is why humans snack constantly. This is why they relentlessly open insolvent restaurants and invest hours into conversations over where to get brunch. Humans are constantly searching for any meager scrap of life they can jam down their gullet. The average human is (of course) not conscious of this desire. The desire is invisible. But it's still inherent to who that human is. The hunger for life is always present. There's a reason toddlers are driven to eat dirt. Dirt contains microbes, and microbes are alive. The craving to consume the living earth is something we train ourselves to unlearn. Only a child intuits that dirt is a good thing to eat.

The reason the truth about food remains unknown is (I assume) obvious to everyone. The researchers all understood that this kind of knowledge could not be published. Society could not handle this depth of reinvention. We're not going to start climbing ladders and eating apples off their branches, nor are we going to stop pretending that what we currently put in our mouths has any impact on how we feel. Some things can't be changed. We are animals, but not that kind of animal. We are not healthy, but we are healthy enough.

Every Day Just
Comes and Goes

HIS HUSBAND ALWAYS CALLED IT THE LAKE, WHICH DROVE HIM berserk. They both knew what it was. They both knew it was a reservoir. It had been described as a reservoir by the realtor, on the first day they looked at the house. It didn't even resemble a lake, except for the water. You could see the goddamn concrete. "Call it what it is. Quit acting like it's pretentious to use the word *reservoir*. People know you're pretending not to know the difference. It's not amusing to be wrong on purpose. People hate that more than pretension."

These were Trevor's thoughts as he ran along the artificial shoreline, past the half-empty dog park and the desolate basketball courts, struggling to complete an aerobic 4.4-mile jaunt before the sun turned ultra-oppressive. Marital annoyance was his last cogent notion, before the confrontation.

He first saw the man from a distance. The man stood in the middle of the path, neither walking nor running, hands on hips. He wasn't dressed for the conditions. He didn't look dangerous, but he also didn't look like the kind of person Trevor wanted to encounter at random, since there was no kind of person Trevor wanted to encounter at random. He tacked to his right, preparing to pass without eye contact. But then the man spoke, and he was forced to glance over.

"Trevor," said the man in a three-piece suit. "Trevor Pepper."

Trevor stopped, his auburn beard loaded with sweat from the heat and mucus from his allergies. He removed his earbuds and looked at a man he did not recognize. "Do I know you?" asked Trevor. They were roughly the same age, so it was possible they were already acquainted. It was becoming progressively difficult to remember whom he had and hadn't met. His memory had changed after his thirtieth birthday. His head was running out of RAM.

"Yes," said the man in the suit. "We've met. But not yet."

Trevor was not in the mood for riddles. He was never in the mood for riddles and didn't like people who were. His options, however, were limited. He could have just kept running, which would have been rude, or he could have politely asked the man to leave him alone, which was potentially ruder. But the stranger kept talking, so Trevor was trapped.

"Can you come with me? I have a vehicle nearby."

"No," said Trevor. "I'm not going anywhere, with you or anyone else. Why would I do that?"

"Would you be willing to walk around the reservoir with me? We will walk and talk," said the man. "I have two bottles of water."

"No," said Trevor. "I don't want to do that."

"But I need to tell you something," said the man.

"Then tell me now."

The man moved closer to Trevor, casually holding up his palms as a gesture of peace. Trevor balled his right hand into a fist, just in case.

"I need to tell you two things, both of which are significant," said the man in the suit. "In order for you to accept the second point—which is the more important point—I need to start by telling you the first point, which is that I know everything about you."

"Fantastic," said Trevor dispassionately, already losing interest. The stranger, however, was not lying. He did know everything there was to know about Trevor, and he proved it in less than ninety seconds. He knew everything about Trevor's family and everything about Trevor's career. He knew the layout of Trevor's childhood home. He knew that Trevor's favorite movie was *The Shining*, even though Trevor always told people it was *Barry Lyndon*. He knew graphic details about his sex life, though he framed these details as respectful compliments. He knew a secret Trevor had kept his whole life regarding a flashlight he'd stolen from a church rectory when he was seven, a private shame Trevor had buried so deep in his memory that he'd almost convinced himself it was something he'd read in a book. He knew abstract things about Trevor's political ideology that felt intuitively true, even though Trevor could not recall having ever voiced such abstractions aloud.

"I get it," said Trevor, stopping the man as he described the Pink Floyd poster a fake girlfriend had once given him on Good Friday. "I get it. I mean, obviously I don't *get it* get it, because what you're doing is impossible. But I get that something impossible is happening, and that it's happening to me. So tell me the second thing you need to tell me. Let's get this over with."

"That reaction," said the smiling stranger, "is the reason I'm here. Who else could so easily handle this kind of revelation? Who else would readily accept the impossible? Only you. That's why you're necessary."

"Don't patronize me," said Trevor. "Get on with your business."

"You already know why I'm here," said the man.

"Actually I have no idea, and you're not making any sense, and this is neither interesting nor charming, and I'm not traveling through time," said Trevor. "I have no desire for any of this."

The stranger rolled his owlish eyes.

"Now really, Trevor," said the man. "Why would you possibly jump to that conclusion? What would possibly generate that mental leap? You clearly comprehend what's happening here. If I know all these things about your life, these things that I could only learn firsthand from you, a man I've supposedly never met—I mean, come on. You're smart. This conversation could only happen if it had already happened before."

"Nope," said Trevor. "Not interested. Whatever this is, I'm not interested."

"Trevor, we are going to travel four hundred forty years into the future. I'm going with you. We're going together. There is no other way."

"Nope."

"Trevor, this is important. Nothing is more important than this."

"There is no way I'm traveling through time. Unless you can make it happen against my will, which you can't. Because why would we have this conversation if you could?"

"Trevor, be practical."

"I don't want to travel into the future. Why would I want that?"

"The reason you were selected is increasingly self-evident," replied the man in the suit. "And if I told you why we must do this, you'd never accept the offer. No rational person would. So I can't tell you why we need to do what we need to do. But I can promise that—when all this is finally over—you will be happy you made the right choice."

"I don't think I'd be happy at all," said Trevor. "I want to be here, and I want it to be now. I'm not some meathead who thinks the world was better in 1973, when rape was hilarious and people said the N-word on network television and you couldn't prove if anything was true or false. And now here you are, and you want me to go how far into the future? Four hundred and forty years? Why? If they're blasting people into the future for unexplained reasons, I assume the future must be awful. I don't need to see a wasteland. I'm not curious about what a dystopia looks like. That future is not my future. That future is your future, and your future is not my problem."

"Here again, Trevor, you seem to be ignoring the only detail that's irrefutable," said the man. "How long must this go on? How many times must we do this? You know you're going to eventually agree. There's no other way we could be talking so calmly about something this complicated, unless you already unconsciously understood something no normal person could possibly comprehend. Which you do. So it's simply a matter of time before your consciousness agrees. Are you telling me it doesn't seem strange that someone you've never met just showed up and started telling you personal facts that only you could know? It doesn't seem curious that you naturally anticipated I was going to ask you to travel through time, even though I never brought that up? Why would that be your first reaction?"

"I'm not your man, man." Trevor pushed the buds back into his ears and loped away, not looking back. He ran hard for a few hundred feet before downshifting back to a trot. He tried not to think about what had just transpired, but his mind couldn't let it go. "That was bizarre," he thought to himself. But then again, maybe not so bizarre. Maybe not. Maybe he'd been too brusque with the stranger. Time travel was theoretically possible, according to the Internet. Supernatural things happened all the time, in places like Russia and Central America. Mathematical probability supports the possibility of aliens. Alternative realities. The multiverse. Wormholes. The fourth dimension. This whole jog around the reservoir could actually be a lucid dream, and he was just realizing that now. Or maybe he'd tripped a few yards back and hit his head on a rock, and this perceived conversation was some sort of neurological event. Maybe he was still in a coma. Maybe the guy was an actor and this had been a setup for some hidden-camera show he would have loved as a teenager. "Only in L.A.," he said to himself, involuntarily smiling. Were they still making those practical joke shows? He hadn't seen one in a while, but there were so many channels now. Also, it was getting danger-ously warm. He was feeling dehydrated, and the heat plays with your mind. He looked out across the water. The surface was so stagnant it looked like a painting. Not a painting he could paint, of course. A paint-ing by someone who knew how to paint. If Trevor painted that water, it wouldn't look anything like the way it actually was. But why feel bad about his inability to paint? He'd never tried painting in his life. He'd tried photography, for a while, when he was twenty-one. But photography was entirely digital now, and less of a skill than it used to be. He'd always been taught that a photographer earned his reputation in the darkroom. But now darkrooms didn't even exist. Maybe he could build one in his unfinished basement and buy an old Kodak camera and get back into it, although he'd probably lose interest after six months, just like he had in college.

Trevor completed his 4.4-mile lap and returned to his home, every thread of his clothing drenched with perspiration. He stripped off his clothes as he walked through the house, beelining for the outdoor shower ensconced in the backyard. "How was the lake?" asked his husband. Trevor winced.

"Good," said Trevor. "Hot."

"No kidding. Was anyone else even out there?"

"Nobody," said Trevor.

"You're dedicated," he said. "It's admirable."

"I do what I can," said Trevor. He stepped through the sliding glass door and strolled to the shower, invisible to the world, nude and relaxed and confused.

Blizzard of Summer

THE MEETING WAS CALLED BY THE MANAGER, THOUGH THE SINGER and the keyboardist had essentially demanded he do so. The guitarist had no idea what was happening. The drummer assumed it had something to do with the upcoming tour. The bassist didn't show up at all. The DJ wasn't an official member of the group, but she showed up anyway because she had nothing better to do.

The manager was too old to be working with a band like this. He was too old to be working with musicians who still argued about what kind of haircuts would make them look like they weren't concerned with their appearance. He didn't even like the group's music, though he never said that directly. For the past two years, he had unsuccessfully tried to convince them to alter their sound, incessantly pushing them away from power pop and toward metal or ska, two genres he perceived as having greater audience loyalty. But now the group was breaking, finally, and for a reason no one could have anticipated: The song "Blizzard of Summer," recorded for the band's debut album and never released as a proper single, was suddenly the sixth-most popular download in North America. Without promotion or radio airplay, it had become an underground smash. They had offers from all the major festivals and several touring supergroups, one of which would be playing stadiums in Australia. This was (almost) real success. But there was also an emerging problem, which was why this meeting was called.

"I'm going to cut to the chase," said the manager as he vaped. "The following issue was brought to my attention by Barb and Paul two days ago, although I'd already noticed a few curious things on social media before they contacted me. Certainly, we're all pretty pleased, and I suppose a bit surprised, by what's been happening with 'Blizzard of Summer.' But there is also this other aspect, this other trajectory, that's becoming increasingly discomfiting, and I know Barb and Paul feel like it needs to be addressed. I'm not sure I necessarily agree with them on this point, but—"

"How can you not agree?" asked Barb, cutting him off at the pass. "With what part of this do you disagree?"

"I suppose I'm a little concerned that addressing it publicly will only make it worse," said the manager. "It's not like this is a widely known thing. To some degree, this is about optics."

"Optics? Which optics?" asked Corey, softly noodling on an unplugged guitar. "Is this about the record sounding thin? If people are saying it's a little thin, I fucking agree. We should go back and re-record the overdubs. I think if I moved back to some medium eleven gauges, or maybe even thicker, the tone would be where we want it."

"No one is complaining about the thinness of the record," said Paul. "No one is worried about the gauge of your guitar strings."

"Then what the fuck are we worried about?"

The manager was not sure how to explain this to Corey, a guy who believed unicorns were real animals that had gone extinct during the Ice Age. Even Dana, the drummer, thought Corey was stupid, and Dana was the type of person who thought Drake memes were subversive. Still, the manager had to try, so he tried: "Blizzard of Summer" was a track Barb and Paul had written about the end of their romantic relationship, a rupture that had occurred around the same time the band was forming. In truth, their love affair had always been tepid and contrived. Many of their peers suspected their only motive for falling in love was so that they could eventually break up and fabricate a micro version of Fleetwood Mac's *Rumours*. The central riff on "Blizzard of Summer" was a synthesis of Hole's "Celebrity Skin" and the opening theme to *Sesame Street*. It was supposed to be a melancholy song that sounded happy on the surface, a little like something by the Carpenters, but the words were so indistinct that any underlying darkness was invisible. The title of the song was never used in the lyrics. It was written in a 4/4 time signature. It was exactly three minutes long. And for reasons that were impossible to isolate, racists seemed to love it.

Not since Skrewdriver's 1983 single "White Power" had a song resonated so overwhelmingly with racist consumers of mainstream pop. It was a runaway alt-right banger (Richard Spencer had supposedly worn one of the band's T-shirts while delivering a speech advocating the use of chemical weapons in Mexico). An instrumental bluegrass version of the track was recently performed at a Ku Klux Klan rally in Indiana. Most perplexing was a capsule review of "Blizzard of Summer" in the Stormfront-sponsored music publication *Modern Xenophobe*, where culture writer Wolfgang Wallace noted that he begrudgingly loved the song's fascist ideology despite disliking the composition of the music, a dissonance that contradicted his philosophy as a formalist critic. Barb and Paul first suspected something was amiss while doing press for their upcoming remix album, when multiple radio hosts queried their thoughts on the 1964 Civil Rights Act. They were equally disturbed by a demographic chart illustrating where "Blizzard of Summer" had been most aggressively streamed and downloaded: The deepest saturation coagulated around South Boston, although the track was also inordinately popular in Serbia.

"I'm not sure how we proceed here," said the manager. He conceded that this was not an issue he'd dealt with before. "I think the first thing we should do is establish our baseline position. Barb and Paul have already expressed their views. But just so we're all on the same page: Is everybody in this band against racism? Could I safely put out a press release stating that no member of the group is a white supremacist?"

"I am not a white supremacist," said the drummer.

"I am not a white supremacist," said Corey. "And even if I was, I don't like labels."

"I am not a white supremacist," said the DJ. "And I think that should probably go without saying, since I'm black."

"Okay, great," said the manager. "We've established a clear political identity. I think the next move is to figure out how and why this happened."

This, it seemed, was unfathomable. The band fundamentally agreed on one point: If oppressed minorities viewed the song as racist, then it was, in fact, accidentally racist. But that did not seem to be the case. No one had accused "Blizzard of Summer" of being pejoratively offensive. No one found it hateful or problematic. The only people who viewed it as racist were white people who thought racism was awesome. The lyrics made no references to white nationalism. The song's subtext was vague and possibly nonexistent. The manager noted that the title did include the word *blizzard*, and blizzards are made of snow, and snow is white. But Paul was quick to admit that this was a reference to Barb's temporary cocaine addiction. Corey rhetorically asked if Paul and Barb had possibly broken up over a racial argument, and if it was possible that the emotion of the dispute had infiltrated the texture of the song in a manner so understated that it could only be sensed by unusually perceptive racists. However, the value of his hypothesis was undercut by his second theory, which was that the problem could be solved with the addition of a solo reminiscent of early Jeff Beck.

The band was at a crossroads, and not the kind of crossroads you want. This crossroads did not involve Robert Johnson, Steve Vai, or Britney Spears. Barb wanted to stop playing "Blizzard of Summer" altogether, even if it cratered their career. Paul agreed with Barb, but added that it wasn't that simple (and that maybe they *should* play the song, under the right circumstances, as a way to reclaim its power). Corey thought they should continue playing it at every show, but that they should augment the set with a cover of Bob Marley's "No Woman, No Cry." The drummer said he would do whatever everyone else wanted. The DJ didn't get a vote, nor did she want one.

"We're dealing with a fundamental question about art," the manager finally said, trying to sound like a person who understood the problem. "Does the motive of the artist matter, or is the received message the only thing that counts? Two of you wrote a love song. Some people think it's a hate song. Smart people get it. Dumb people don't. But dumb people are still people. We can't discount the taste of dumb people. That's half the audience. Half the people who loved the Beatles were idiots. Charles Manson thought the song 'Helter Skelter' was about a coming race war. It's actually about a British carnival slide. But nobody got murdered because ten million people didn't think 'Helter Skelter' was about racial genocide. People got murdered because one person thought that it was. So again, this is about optics. We need to weigh the value of many normal people understanding the song in a shallow way, against the risk of a few abnormal people misunderstanding the song in a profound way."

They all sat for a moment, saying nothing. Paul broke the silence.

"We really need to get Hank's thoughts on this," he said. Hank was the bass player. "Why isn't he here? What's he doing?"

"He's back at the hotel," said the drummer. "He's working on a new song. I've heard a little bit of it, and it's good. Almost a power ballad. It's apparently about his parents' divorce, although I would have never figured that out if he hadn't told me."

"That's wonderful," said Barb. "Hank is usually so reticent to write anything personal. This is a big step forward for him. What's the song called?"

"He told me the working title is 'Bomb Israel.' But maybe we'll want to retool that."

Of Course It Is

THIS IS NOT THE WAY I'M SUPPOSED TO DO THIS. I GET THAT. I ALSO know I'm not supposed to admit that I know I'm doing it wrong, as that compounds the original mistake. I don't care. The objective here is not elegance or craft. I don't want to waste your time. I'm just going to start.

I wake up this morning with nothing to do. The only thing I know for certain is that I don't need to go to work. What do I do for living? I can't recall. But I look out the bedroom window and the weather is ideal, by which I mean ideal for me specifically. It's either early spring or late fall. Do I find it odd that I don't know the season? I do not. You can see where this is going. It's almost eleven, so I take a hot shower and throw on a green sweater and walk to the Chinese restaurant around the corner. Everything on the menu is cheap, almost to the point of parody. It's like a menu from before I was born. I order four different entrees, and they're all slightly better than I expect. I bus my tray and start walking back to my apartment, but I pick up the scent of sandalwood incense wafting from a street-level window. Some doomed entrepreneur has opened a record store right next to my building. It's a terrible location for a retail outlet and there's no way it will survive, but the selection is incredible.

They have a live bootleg of Jimi Hendrix playing with Miles Davis in Stockholm, on vinyl. They have a soundtrack Black Sabbath recorded in 1974 for a never-released animated film about Genghis Khan. I buy nine or ten albums and drop them off at my apartment, a third-floor walk-up that's clean and organized and smells like oranges. I head back outside and stroll to the darkest bar within walking distance. It's empty in that way bars are always empty in the late afternoon. The muted TV is rebroadcasting an NBA game from the night before. The score is tied, the fourth quarter is just starting, and Rajon Rondo already has sixteen assists. I watch the game and drink draft beer from a glass mug that's been stored in the freezer. My growing level of intoxication is synchronized with the setting of the sun. The bartender looks like Winona Ryder's taller, Catholic sister. She's a graduate student in political science. We talk about H. Ross Perot's impact on the 1992 presidential election and why pancakes are superior to waffles. Her favorite comedian is Neil Hamburger. She sells me drugs and I leave without saying goodbye. When I get home, there's some leftover beef stew in the fridge, which I couldn't possibly have cooked and which contains spices I've never previously encountered. I go to bed early and it starts to rain.

Now, I don't need to tell you what's happening here. That would be insulting to you, and maybe to me. It's obvious to both of us. There's a certain genre of story that's always the same, and this is one of those stories. In no way am I trying to blow your mind. You get it. I get it. We all get it.

There is, however, one aspect here that warrants examination, and I'd love your feedback on this point, although that's impossible for many reasons, chiefly the fundamental illogic of this document's very existence. But here again, let's not waste our energy with something as worthless as logic. I'm just going to get into it.

What's the only thing we all know about every variation of this particular scenario? What's the one thing that's *always* true, the one thing that *must* be true, in order for this scenario to have any meaning at all? It is, in simplest terms, the telegraphing of the twist: It has to be that the individual at the center of the experience initially assumes he's in some version of heaven, only to realize he's actually in his own version of hell. I fully accept that this must be what's happening to me. Every day, I wake up with nothing to do. I have a gratuitous lunch, I flip through a bunch of records that can't be real, I get drunk in the afternoon, I talk to multiple incarnations of a female bartender who's a projection of my most sophomoric desires, and I find some surprise stew in the best possible rendering of my kitchen. How many times has this occurred? No idea. Rondo is always playing for the Dallas Mavericks, so I must have died in the vicinity of 2015. But I'm also not sure if a "day" in this reality is twenty-four hours. Sometimes I get the sense that this has happened to me hundreds of thousands of times, even though I never remember the previous day. I'm always surprised by everything that happens, every single time. It's only at the very end, when I'm lying under a gravity blanket I've never purchased and listening to the rain, that it gradually dawns on me that I'm operating inside some perpetual post-existence loop I won't recognize when I wake up tomorrow morning. Which, based on every short story I read in junior high and every *Twilight Zone* episode I've ever watched, is the moment I'm supposed to be overcome with the existential terror of my imprisonment.

Except that last part never happens.

I just fall asleep and forget.

Sometimes I briefly think, "Maybe this *is* heaven. Maybe that's the twist on the twist." But that can't be right. Things aren't *that* awesome. I buy interesting records but I never get to hear them. I never have sex with the bartender. I like stew, but I wouldn't order it at a restaurant. It's a pretty banal paradise. I suppose an argument could be made for the sensation of anticipation; maybe what makes a person happiest is imagining all the music they have yet to hear and fantasizing about all the sex they have yet to have. Maybe my stomach likes stew more than my mind is willing to admit. Still, I know what I know. I'm just not getting an Elysium vibe from any of this. It's mystical, but low-grade mystical. One way or the other, this has to be a projection of whatever used to be my consciousness. And if that's where the projection originates, the internal rules of its consequence must come from the same source, which is my own brain. And my brain knows this scenario can only have one explanation: I am dead, and I am in hell. This *must* be hell, and I must deserve to be here. So what am I doing wrong? Where is the torment? Can't I do anything right?

The fact that I'm in hell is surprising, but I wouldn't call it shocking. I can't remember the person I was when I was alive, so I can't assert that I didn't do terrible things. Maybe I burned villages. Maybe I died while torturing a baby sloth. That, however, is almost beside the point. If I was anything like the post-person I am now, I'd have operated from the position that hell probably doesn't exist, but if it does, it's a place where almost no one goes or where almost everyone goes. The fact that this was the full extent of my spiritual perspective would likely be enough to place me in the second category. Sometimes I wonder if perhaps I was a completely different guy when I was alive, with a wife and kids, and my eternal separation from those people is the crux of my castigation. I can't remember any wife and I can't remember any kids, yet this feeling persists. It's (almost) troubling. But of course, I only have these nagging thoughts when I'm falling asleep, and only if I choose to fixate on the possibility that I'm missing some critical clue within this otherwise pleasant eternity. I never feel sad. Never. Annoyed, sometimes, but never despondent. One night I had this breakthrough vision that I must be in purgatory and that the moment I finally embrace my sadness will be the same moment I ascend into heaven. The only problem is that you can't make yourself sad without the benefit of personal memory, and I can't even remember my name without looking at my driver's license. Plus, if purgatory is a Chinese restaurant and a record store and a decent bar, heaven might just be a shopping mall in Minneapolis. Plus, this is not purgatory, because this is hell, because of course it is.

I once read something (I can't remember where or when) that claimed the hardest work a soul could do was to be aware. It strikes me as strange that I can remember this specific line, and that my inexplicable memory of that sentiment must mean something vital (in light of my current situation). The thought has occurred to me that intellectually realizing I'm secretly in hell might be the definition of hell itself, just as this thought has likely occurred to you. Part of me wants this to be true. I like the idea of things being the way they're supposed to be, even if the outcome contradicts my own self-interest. Consistency matters. But that's not how it is. My soul is not working hard. It's not working at all. It's aware of nothing. This is just how I am.

Time to sleep. Talk again tomorrow, or not.

Skin

IT WAS THE BEST RESTAURANT IN THE CITY, ASSUMING YOU BELIEVED the reviews, which are a terrible thing to believe. Reviews dwell on the ancillary—the atmosphere, the service, the presentation. Logan only cared about the food. The food needed to be incredible. But what can you do? Reviews are all you have, so he made a reservation for Plaza 221 at eight o'clock.

They met at the bar. Logan showed up early and Gwen arrived on time. It was tense. There was no illusion of normalcy. Gwen didn't want to look at Logan's face and kept pretending to notice other things. They were soon seated in the middle of the crowded restaurant, just as Logan had requested. The lighting was dim, the table was wide, the menu was abstruse. They'd never been to a place this posh.

"You should get the duck," said Logan. "They say the duck is the best meal in town. They say the skin is a meal unto itself." Gwen ordered the duck. Logan chose the salmon. He insisted they both get pumpkin soup, and some oysters, and a shrimp cocktail to share, and maybe the pot stickers. "Don't worry about the price," urged Logan. He even considered selecting the second most expensive bottle of wine, but then he remembered that expensive white wine sometimes tastes like expired antibiotics, so he opted instead for the second cheapest. Gwen drank most of her glass in two swallows and immediately refilled the goblet.

"Why are we here?" she asked. "Why didn't we go to Olive or Bucky's?" They had gone to Olive at least once a month for over a year. They went to Bucky's when Olive was crowded and they were out of ideas.

"Don't worry about it," said Logan. "Wait until the duck arrives."

It took forty minutes. The service was slow by design. Every time Gwen tried to start a normal conversation, Logan commented on how delicious the appetizers were. He wasn't necessarily wrong, but a tad unconvincing. He overplayed his hand. Gwen was relieved when the duck finally arrived.

"Look at that duck," he said. "That's a quality bird."

Gwen started to carve a fork-sized slice. Logan stopped her. "The skin," he said. "Try the skin first. That's supposed to be the best part."

She stopped carving and looked straight at him. His tie was colorful and too wide. He used a lot of product in his hair. His smile was asymmetrical. He looked like a loser, but she loved him. He was the loser she loved. She took her fork and ripped off a large chunk of skin. It was crisp and salty, lined on the inside with a thin layer of limpid fat. It dissolved in her mouth.

"How's it going down?" asked Logan. "Overrated or underrated?"

"It's excellent," she said. "It's the best skin I've ever tasted."

"Take a full bite," he said. "See how the skin interplays with the flesh."

She did as requested. What else could she do? It was food. She was eating food. And as she chewed, Logan started his ramble.

"I've been thinking a lot, about everything," he began, trying to replicate the speech he'd rehearsed since New Year's. "Life is complicated. Being in love is complicated. We've been at this a long time. Two years is a long time. I can't even remember what it was like before we started dating. I was different. You were very different. We were going to move in together, and then we didn't. Maybe we should have. Maybe if we'd done that, we'd be less different now. But I feel like if the person I've become met the person you've become, there's no way we'd go on even one date, much less live together. You're always nice to me, but everything I say seems to annoy you. We only have sex when one of us is drunk, and that can't be normal. I used to hate being alone. Now I love it. We don't even watch the same TV shows anymore. I don't like your friends and you don't want me to have any friends at all. We probably do still love each other, maybe even more than we did when things were good. But not in the way old married people are supposed to love each other, and it's been two years, and we're not getting younger and we're not getting married. So I want to get out of this, and I think you want the same."

Gwen did not disagree with anything Logan said, except the part about her not wanting him to have friends (although she understood why he thought that, as many of his closest friends were degenerate gamblers). Their relationship wasn't awful, but it was boring, and not in a way that doubled as reassuring. She had indeed become a different person, and so had he. Gwen was a different person because she'd finished graduate school and lost her mother to leukemia. Logan was a different person because he'd installed SiriusXM radio in his car. There wasn't much about him she'd miss, or even remember. Still, two years is a long time to spend with someone you'll never see again. He knew everything about her, and now she'd have to find someone new and retell all the same stories. Logan had always been sweet to her, especially at the funeral. She'd never been this intricately intertwined with another person. Being unsatisfied was a lot of work.

She began to cry, quietly. Quietly, but obviously.

"Wait," said Logan. "What are you doing?"

"What am I doing? What do you think I'm doing?"

"You're crying," he said. "You're crying."

"No shit."

"But . . . the duck?"

And here is where we see the problem with Logan and Gwen, and the larger problem with Logan, and the still larger problem with people who want simple things to be true. Logan had heard an interview. He was driving to Home Depot to buy a hacksaw, and he heard a radio interview with a psychologist who explained how there are certain combinations of things that humans cannot do simultaneously. You can't sneeze with your eyes open, this psychologist explained. You can try, but there's a biological protection drive that will stop it from happening. It's built into our nervous system. You can't sing a song aloud while simultaneously remembering the melody to a different song. You can't experience orgasm while you vomit (it can happen right after or right before, but not concurrently). You can multiply two-digit numbers in your head if you're juggling three objects, but not if you're juggling five objects. The mental multitasking is too extreme. And you cannot, this educated man on the radio explained, begin weeping while tasting something new and delicious. People with eating disorders often eat *while* they're crying, but that's not the same thing—the crying happens before they start or after they've finished. Within that express moment of ecstatic gustatory inception, the psychologist claimed, a human's tear ducts mechanically block themselves. To Logan, this was a revelation. He did not want to be with Gwen. He did not want to spend time with her, or take responsibility for his laziness, or meet her friends at wine bars with limited menus, or remember nonessential holidays, or get criticized for wearing shoes that were no longer in fashion, or think about any sociopolitical issue that did not directly impact his own day-to-day life. He wanted to disappear, and if that was impossible, he wanted her to disappear. But he did not want to see her cry. Nothing made him feel worse. He would do anything to keep that from happening, and—at long last—he'd found a way. The radio explained everything. It was so simple. All he had to do was tell her the bad news at the same moment she was eating something she loved for the first time. He spent hours reading menus on the Internet, eventually stumbling upon word of this duck skin. The perfect solution, or so it appeared. But here he was, spending a week's pay at Plaza 221, and Gwen was still crying, no differently than if he'd told her the news in her own goddamn bathroom. Why had he believed that radio psychologist? Why did he assume the psychologist was credible? He couldn't even remember the man's name, or if he'd ever known it at all. And he couldn't apologize for believing him, because that would mean he'd need to explain his plan, which he now realized was stupid, and which Gwen would view as even stupider than it actually was. And then she would be crying *and* angry, which was the only thing worse than crying.

"I'm sorry," he said. "I guess I just expected you to enjoy the duck."

It might not be so terrible to start again, Gwen thought to herself. It might be easy.

The Perfect Kind
of Friend

I VALUE MY FRIENDS MORE THAN I SHOULD. IT'S A WEAKNESS. PEOPLE have told me this in the past and I can never prove them wrong. Every rebuttal falls flat, so I just pretend to be happy about it. I pretend like it's a good thing. My friends have more control over my life than they possibly realize. No matter how much I like them, I want them to like me more. If they don't, I live in fear that they'll lose interest in our rapport and pursue other, deeper friendships with other, deeper people. I spend an inordinate amount of time nurturing relationships that provide no satisfaction to either party. This includes relationships with people I don't know.

Seven years ago, I was struggling with a series of questions. These were not practical questions, nor were they associated with some higher intellectual goal. These were thoughts made of cement that occupied my mind against its will, motivated by forces I chose not to control. These forces were drugs. I had become disenchanted with my drug of choice. My tolerance had grown too high. I felt as though I needed to find a heavier drug for day-to-day use. But this thought was countered by an opposing thought of equal value: Did the fact that I was considering such a move prove that my tolerance was weaker than I believed? Would only a heavily intoxicated person deliberately pursue a more serious addiction, simply because their current addiction had become predictable? Would only a high person worry they were not high enough, in the same way only a drunk believes they need more to drink?

It occurred to me that I knew at least one person who could solve this puzzle: my quasi-friend Todd Kilmer, an author who'd recently published *Zowzow Wowzow*, an acclaimed 716-page book on the psychosomatic history of recreational drug abuse. "What wonderful friends I have," I thought to myself as I typed a solipsistic multipronged query into my phone. Here I was, relaxing on my porch at midnight, listening to the distant bark of an unseen dog, quarantined inside my own insular world. Yet through the power of technology, my fears could be addressed by an expert in the field. A man living in London, thousands of miles away, would tell me things about myself I could not learn on my own, instantly and without cost. Our dialogue would be more than an exchange of information. It would be an exchange of emotional currency. It would serve as human connecting fluid. Todd Kilmer would be flattered by my question and I would be educated by his diagnosis. It would galvanize our quasi-friendship without requiring either of us to do anything remotely inconvenient.

But I made a mistake.

My mistake (if this can technically be classified as such) is that I'm also quasi-acquainted with a different person named Tom Kilnard, who I don't actually know. Our lives collided by chance, in a community I lived in for less than a year, so long ago that I can't recall how old I was at the time of our meeting. We shared a mutual associate, or maybe we voted in the same precinct, or maybe we briefly played softball together. I cannot recount our origin story. I cannot recall the details of his face or the timbre of his voice. I don't know if he was tall or short. But I do know this: I once needed a ride to the airport, and Tom Kilnard offered to drive me, assuming he wasn't working or on a date or watching something he liked on TV. That ride never came to fruition. I took a cab. His offer had seemed a little soft. But the offer was nonetheless discussed, and phone digits were traded, and names were cataloged into contact lists. And now, three phones later, he exists for the sole purpose of punishing the inaccuracy of my thumb. So on this night, on my porch, I do not text my solipsistic multipronged question to author Todd Kilmer. I text my solipsistic multipronged question to Tom Kilnard, the human equivalent of a character from a dream that has already begun to dissolve. I send my question to a friend who is not my friend. But the message is received, and the message is absorbed. And over the next nine minutes, I receive fifteen consecutive messages from Tom Kilnard.

He is not, for whatever reason, surprised to hear from me.

"Great that you reached out," read his opening volley. The sentence did not end with a period or an exclamation mark. This is important. A 2015 academic study from Binghamton University argued that unpunctuated texts indicate sincerity, as sincere people don't text with punctuation. His following fourteen missives were similarly fragmented and unpolished. Most involved autocorrect errors. Their lengths varied dramatically, and his prose style was akin to that of a panda. It would be uncouth of me to reprint these texts verbatim. That would be unkind to Tom Kilnard, and I am not a gossip. But here is the gist, interpreted in sequence, encapsulated cogently, minus certain incriminating details:

> Your concerns are valid, and you are brave to have expressed them.

> I, too, have tangled with problems of illicit desire.

My wife, she does not understand me. When we fell in love, there were albums and films we both enjoyed equally. Now she has no interest in any of those things. It is as if she's no longer a person, replaced by a bloodless humanoid with whom I am forced to cohabitate.

This issue is not really about albums and films, however. It never is.

There are things in life I need, and I could not get them from my spouse. I was compelled to pursue them through the Internet.

I began to have affairs.

My initial affairs were anonymous and fleeting. Purely physical. Deliberately empty. Over time, I began to desire indiscriminate sexual encounters that provided the chimera of emotional investment. Later, these affairs became entirely emotional, with only the hypothetical promise of sex, never to be consummated. But this was not enough.

Like you, I found myself unsatisfied with the degree to which I could escape from reality. I longed for intensity, but intensity without commitment. Auto-erotic asphyxiation became a pastime. I would check into hotel rooms to hang myself while masturbating. I read a lot about the dead singer from INXS. It turns out that was just a normal suicide. The media got it wrong.

I pursued opportunities for group sex. I engaged in an orgy at a karaoke bar. I would enter gay clubs and experiment with dalliances that did not organically arouse me. I would attempt to seduce professional women I had met only moments before, sometimes in a retail or banking capacity, overtly proposing intercourse in a nearby public lavatory. I was surprised that it worked on two different occasions.

Yet this was still not enough. [*This was a very long, somewhat repetitive text.*]

Perhaps I was not like other people. Perhaps the rules of society did not apply to me. [*This text, in its original form, included some marginally disturbing content.*]

I watched a documentary about a group of men arrested for making love to a horse. I watched another documentary about people who choose to have sex inside garbage dumpsters. These were not things I wanted to do. But then why did I sometimes find myself fantasizing about horses and garbage, even as I engaged in traditional sex with strangers? Was normal physicality no longer enough?

I eventually told my wife. I told her everything. She admitted she had suspicions and that something in our marriage was amiss. I offered to enter a clinic for sex addiction. But as we discussed this option, I noticed something peculiar: My wife was paradoxically intrigued by the depraved stories I perfunctorily recounted. She was disgusted, but also excited.

My wife, it seems, had secrets of her own.

This fourteen-text exchange, as noted previously, occurred seven years ago. There were so many reasonable things I could have done: not respond at all, apologize for texting the wrong person, feign mild interest before disappearing forever. Yet I did none of those things. I returned Tom Kilnard's texts, thanking him for his candor. I told him his secrets had helped me, which was (maybe) two percent true. I urged him to keep me updated about his life, and of course he has. He texts me his darkest thoughts, constantly. He texts me about the twisted transgressive sex games his wife now initiates, about the lives they have ruined and enriched, about the square people at his office who know nothing of his sex-positive perversions. My guarded replies are brief and facile, but always prompt. "Fascinating," I type. "Tell me more." He rarely tells me anything I want to know. He more often tells me things I wish I couldn't remember. I would never want to encounter him, or even see him from a distance. But it's been a wonderful seven years. It's been a wonderful seven years, learning about this man I could not pick out of a police lineup. He wants this more than I do. He needs this more than I do. He's exactly like me, except a million times worse. The perfect kind of friend.

Cat Person

W E'RE NOT CALLING THIS ASSJACK A SERIAL KILLER," THE chief of police said for the third time in as many minutes. "For starters, it's not accurate. But even if it were, we would never say that it was. Once the media hears those words, it's over. It doesn't matter how we sell it."

"But it's a man killing people at random," said McMullin. "Or at least a man who's trying to kill people at random."

"We don't know that," said the chief. "We don't know what he's trying to do."

"Yes we do," said McMullin. "If you're so unclear about what's happening, why are we using the serial killer task force?"

"Don't call it that," said the chief. "Do not use that term. We're implementing an investigative task force for the purpose of anonymous suspect profiling. And when you talk to your little buddy from the *Post*, that's what you will say."

"She's not a toddler," said McMullin. "She's going to know what those words mean."

"That's on her," said the chief. "She can write what she wants. But if I see the words *serial killer*, they better not be inside a quote."

"Or what? Will you tell me I'm off the case? Why are you talking like a TV cop?"

"You're fucking Irish. You're the cliché here," said the chief. "Now go out and do something useful."

McMullin left the precinct a few minutes before six and took the Metrorail Red Line to Unseld's, the only bar where he felt comfortable talking to a woman who wasn't his wife. He'd told Lola he'd be there by six-thirty and assumed he'd be early, but she was already waiting, reading her phone and drinking Diet Coke. Tomorrow at noon there'd be a press conference and all this peculiarity would be public, but McMullin always talked to Lola a day early. She would get to break the story in return for shaping what all the other reporters would feel obligated to ask. This was their unspoken agreement. It had been this way for years.

"What do you have?" asked Lola. There was never any need for hellos.

"It's a goofy one," said McMullin. "Let me get a drink first."

He walked to the bar, ordered a Greyhound, and internally rehearsed what he was about to explain. He wanted to be truthful without being honest. He trusted Lola, but only to the extent any reasonable police officer would trust any credible journalist. Just before he turned around, he ordered a second Greyhound, for Lola. Maybe she'd take it and maybe she wouldn't. But it would always be better if he could say they'd both been drinking, in case he made a mistake.

"There's a short version and a long version," he said upon his return to the booth. "Here's the short version: We've created an investigative task force with the express function of profiling an unknown person of interest. The suspect is a white male using organic objects to expose unsystematic victims to a *Toxoplasma gondii* infection. We don't know what his motive is."

"Jesus," said Lola. "Biological terrorism. Is Homeland Security involved?"

"Oh no," said McMullin, legitimately surprised. "Don't write that. Don't even imply that. You're way off base. I get why you'd mentally go there, but no. This isn't terrorism. There's no activist aspect. It's not political. This is just a man rubbing cats on people."

"Pardon?"

"Yeah. I know."

"Can you elaborate?"

"Can we go off-the-record for a bit?"

Lola nodded her head, turned off the tape recorder, and placed her pen next to the untouched Greyhound. McMullin tried to act casual as he told her what he knew, which was as much as anyone knew. Two months ago, a twenty-four-year-old woman went to a tanning salon on D Street. She put on a bikini and climbed into a tanning bed. She closed her eyes and lost track of time. But then the lid of the tanning bed unexpectedly opened, and before she could even speak or react, a stranger wearing sunglasses started rubbing a shorthaired orange cat against her exposed stomach. She screamed and the man fled, escaping through a fire exit with a disconnected alarm. The incident was reported, and there was a brief debate over whether the attack should be classified as a sexual assault. The woman, seemingly unharmed, was willing to dismiss the event as a "news of the weird" scenario and accepted ten free tanning sessions as compensation. The man with the cat was not pursued. But then, two days later, a similar attack happened to a middle-aged man who'd just finished showering at a local YMCA. While searching the floor of his locker for a pair of trousers, the man felt a furry sensation against his buttocks, accompanied by a series of discomfiting meows. Again, the assailant fled when the victim turned to confront him; again, the incident was not viewed as significant (in the filed report, the victim even requested that his affinity for animals be cited on the record). But in the weeks that followed, something that had once seemed comical grew progressively sociopathic. Across the metro area, dozens of individuals began telling of a white male of average height wearing sunglasses and a hooded sweatshirt who would approach them at inopportune moments and rub an adult orange cat against their face. His modus operandi exhibited no consistent pattern. Victims were unrelated and spanned every demographic. On one occasion, the attacker hid in the backseat of an unlocked vehicle and started rubbing the cat against the neck and head of the driver as he pulled into traffic. Schoolchildren and the elderly were especially vulnerable, since many found the experience unthreatening and pleasant. Many of his victims declined to fight back, usually due to a combination of confusion and an unwillingness to strike the (assumedly innocent) feline. There were now at least sixty-eight people who had been assaulted in this manner, and it was believed the assailant was now using three different cats, including a white Angora.

"That's quite something," Lola said at the story's conclusion. "And I agree that it's absolutely a newsworthy story, for somebody else. But you know what I cover. You know the kinds of stories I like. This seems like a rather adorable crime. How is this a *violent* crime? You made it sound like people were being poisoned or something."

"They are," said McMullin. "Are we still off-the-record?"

The problem, the officer explained, was not that a man was arbitrarily rubbing cats on people. That was merely bizarre. The problem was the cats themselves. They all carried the *Toxoplasma gondii* parasite, and that was no accident.

"I don't know what that is," said Lola. "I'm not a science writer."

"Have you ever heard of someone referred to as a crazy cat lady?" asked McMullin.

"Of course," said Lola. "And that's a highly gendered term. That's offensive."

"I don't disagree," McMullin lied. "But if you know what that means, it means you already know what *Toxoplasma gondii* is."

The *Toxoplasma gondii* parasite is normally no big deal, even among parasites. It can live inside the white blood cells of any mammal and has almost no superficial impact on the host, outside of a brief, mild flu. In Europe, the number of humans who've been exposed to the "toxo" parasite is greater than the number of humans who have not. But certain details about *Toxoplasma gondii* are highly unconventional. One is that the only place the parasite can sexually reproduce is inside the digestive tract of domestic housecats. Another is that rodents infected by *Toxoplasma gondii* lose their innate fear of cats and find themselves paradoxically attracted to the smell of cat urine (which explains the evolutionary advantage for cats to serve as hosts). Still another detail is the ambiguous link between *Toxoplasma gondii* and schizophrenia, bipolar disorder, depression, and overall mental deterioration, which is why some people believe living alone in a house with multiple cats for multiple years can turn an ostensibly sensible woman into a certifiably crazy cat lady.

"Or a crazy cat man," McMullin said at the end of his lecture. "Could just as easily happen to a man."

Lola picked up her pen, clicked the clip three times, and then put it back down. She considered drinking her complimentary Greyhound but decided against it.

"I'm still not seeing this," she said. "This man—he's rubbing cats on people. He's giving people this trivial parasite. But to what end? So that they lose their mind in thirty years?"

"I wish," he said. "We're still off-the-record, right?"

Something had transmogrified, explained McMullin. The toxo parasite unleashed through these cat attacks had been biologically transformed. The version of *Toxoplasma gondii* being transmitted by the assailant was at least twenty times more robust than the *Toxoplasma gondii* found in nature. All its symptoms had amplified and accelerated. Days after that first attack, the twenty-four-year-old woman from the tanning salon had unsuccessfully attempted suicide. The middle-aged man from the YMCA rapidly grew despondent and disappeared from his family without a trace. He was still missing. Almost all of the sixty-eight victims now claimed to be plagued with dark fantasies and an inability to concentrate, often leading to accidents and self-destructive tendencies. A few even described a newfound attraction to the scent of cat piss that bordered on the sexual.

"So this *is* terrorism," said Lola. "That's the definition of what terrorism is. Are you telling me that if the guy with the cats was from Syria, you wouldn't be—"

"Let's not go down that path," said McMullin. "If you want to argue about who society views as a terrorist and who society views as a garden-variety Caucasian maniac, save that debate for the press conference. I mean, if you consider Ted Kaczynski to be a terrorist, then sure. Because that's the type of target we're profiling. We know he has a high IQ. He's probably an academic or a medical lab employee or a vet. We know he loves cats, or that he hates them. We know that he's either immune to the toxo virus or he already has it, and—if he has it—maybe that's what's causing him to attack strangers. But that's all we know. And again, this is all off-the-record."

"What can you tell me on-the-record? Anything?"

"Yes," said McMullin. "We've created an investigative task force for the singular purpose of profiling an unknown person. The person is a white male who wears sunglasses and carries a cat. Citizens should not interact with the cat. The suspect may be exposing victims to an infection, but the infection is traditionally harmless. His reason for doing this is unknown."

"Can I explain why the situation is so unusual?"

"Make it vague," said McMullin. "Don't say the virus has been medically mutated. And don't describe the cat in detail. Don't marginalize orange cats."

Lola said she couldn't write a story without more information, which wasn't true. McMullin said he'd already told her more than he should have, which also wasn't true. Lola begged for one on-the-record detail about how the parasite had been altered. McMullin said, "What parasite?" Lola asked if she could verify any of the off-the-record information through other sources. McMullin told her she could try as long as she didn't mention his name, even though everyone would immediately know she'd received the information from him. It was the same dance they always did.

"I have to go," said Lola. "I have to write this up and then get home to feed my cats."

"How many cats do you have?" asked McMullin.

"Six," she said.

"Oh, wonderful. I hear the cafeteria in the sanitarium is underrated."

"Go fuck yourself in the throat," she replied, and they both smiled.

McMullin left the bar before it got dark. As he walked to the train station, he could see the cherry blossoms in the distance, just starting to bloom. The colors made him wince. Soon the afternoons would be hot. The days would grow humid and miserable. Men would wear khaki shorts. Women would wear tank tops. Exposed skin would be everywhere, and there was nothing he could do about it. The city was a dangerous place.

Experience
Music Project

HOW MANY TIMES DO I HAVE TO REPEAT THIS? I'M ONLY GOING TO tell you the exact same thing I told the other two guys, which is the same thing I told the woman who contacted me originally. I don't understand what my role in this is supposed to be. I'm cooperating. I'm trying to be cooperative. I will continue to cooperate. But this is the last time I'm explaining what I've already explained. You seem pretty chill, and those other two guys were lowkey chill, and that original woman was super chill. I'm trying to be reasonable here. But I still don't get it. I still don't understand the nature of the question.

Like I keep saying: I go to work at noon, every day except Monday and Tuesday. I get off around nine, and I'm usually home by nine-thirty. I do the same thing every night: I get home, I check my email, I change my clothes, and then I take the fire escape up to the roof. I smoke for maybe ten minutes. I take the elevator back down to the lobby and cross the street to the bodega. This is the bodega in question, the one on Smith Street, next to the CVS. I'd never even heard of the word *bodega* until I moved here. We always called them gas stations, but I suppose these places don't sell gas. So I get it. I understand. Words matter. Since the incident, I've started going to the other bodega, the one with the orange cat, way over on Court Street. But that place isn't as good. They don't carry the products I like. No Pepsi products. Only Coke.

But like I keep saying: Back at the place on Smith, there were three different people. Three employees. Sometimes they worked together, but that was rare. Only on Thanksgiving and maybe Christmas Eve. It was typically just one of the three, on some sort of revolving schedule I could never anticipate. There was the guy whose name I couldn't pronounce, the guy who told me I could call him "Jon." There was also the less friendly guy whose name I couldn't pronounce, who was taller and more handsome. And then there was a kid, a teenager, who was younger and whose name I didn't know at all. And like I keep telling you: I don't know what their nationality was, although I assume you people must know, and it's kind of fucked up you won't tell me now, instead of constantly asking me what country they're from and then acting all suspicious when I say I have no idea. I'm bad with accents and I try not to make assumptions. It seems racist to guess who people are. But I don't see why that matters, anyway. If you call me in here again, I want a lawyer. I've seen that episode of *Frontline* about forced confessions. Don't talk to me like I'm a person of interest. I'm not a person of interest. I'm not interesting. All I can tell you is that I sort of knew these three guys, in the sense that I recognized their faces and they recognized mine. I knew Jon the most, because he was talkative. But I didn't *know him* know him. You know? I don't know where he lived or anything about his life. We only talked about one thing, which is the same thing you keep asking about. I'm running out of ways to explain this.

But, okay, fine. Here we go again.

There was a portable stereo system, above the cigarette rack. It looked like a model from the 1980s, except it was brand-new, like it was just out of the box. Pristine. At first, whenever I came into the store, I assumed one of the speakers was blown, because every song I'd hear sounded slightly different than the way I remembered hearing it before, even if the song itself was familiar. Every time I went in there, I'd have this foreign experience with a song I'd heard a thousand times before, particularly when Jon was working, because he only listened to the classic rock station. I'd hear "Hey Nineteen" and it would seem like a totally new song to me. But like I said, I'd just been smoking on the roof, so I didn't always trust my ears. You know what I mean? The first woman told me I could be honest about that. Eventually, I ask Jon about the stereo. I ask if the woofer is busted or if the EQ is set up weird. And he was like, "Oh no, this is just a radio from back home." Here again—I don't know what home he was referring to or where that home was or is, and I didn't ask, since he seemed to act like this was supposed to be obvious. I also didn't care. I don't care about those kinds of details. I was more interested in the stereo than the person. This went on for—I don't know, six months? Nine months? Time is different in the city.

Jon was a dude I liked. A nice, normal dude. Big smile, every time I walked in the door. The fact that I couldn't pronounce his name didn't matter to either of us. He was really into Zeppelin and Cactus and ZZ Top, but his obsession was bands named after geographic locations—Boston, Kansas, Asia, Brownsville Station. He was really into the first Missouri album, which surprised me. But the other guy, the taller handsome guy—he was a difficult kind of dude. He was a little more . . . how would you say it . . . *aloof.* Whenever he was working, he only played the Top 40 station, so it would be, like, Beyoncé and Katy Perry and shit that seemed like dance music. Woman singers. Justin Bieber, probably. The third employee, the youngish kid—he only played rap, and he played it loud. Aggressive rap, like that woman who used to be a stripper and that little nutcase who had all the heart attacks. He played that shit way louder than necessary, this being a place of business. But it sounded kickass in there, even when the music sucked. You'd get some heavy reverb off the Doritos bags.

Now, I know this next part is what you people are obsessed with, so I'll try to be as straightforward as possible: Last Friday, I go in there when Jon is working, and the song on the stereo is "25 or 6 to 4" by Chicago, which of course Jon loves. We talk a little about the way the drums were recorded. I know a lot about drums, for a nondrummer. And then, just to sort of kill time and keep the conversation going, I mention how the taller employee, the handsome aloof guy, always reminded me of the singer from Depeche Mode, and that he was always playing techno. This wasn't exactly true, because techno is never on the radio and I'm not totally sure what the singer from Depeche Mode even looks like anymore. But that was what I said. And Jon laughed *real* hard at that. Like, maybe too hard, in retrospect. It wasn't like what I said was particularly funny. But he laughs and he laughs, and I go home. No big whoop. But then the next night, I'm back in the store, and now the handsome aloof dude is behind the counter, and I notice he's listening to an Imagine Dragons cover of Third Eye Blind, and I stupidly mention the conversation from the previous evening. I stupidly mention the conversation I'd had with Jon, and how this conversation had made Jon laugh. Which clearly annoys him. Maybe it annoys him too much, in retrospect. I try to mend the fence. I say something like, "Oh, don't overreact. Jon just values authenticity and auteurship. He sees traditional rock 'n' roll as the governing state of popular music. His dialectic spectrum does not engage with alternative canons that hope to subvert the white heteronormative view of culture." Honestly, I was just trying to get out of there. Like I said—I barely know the guy.

So then on Sunday, I go in the bodega again, and now it's the third guy working. The teenage rap guy. And it's loud as hell in there, but—for the first time ever—the kid turns down the volume as I pay for my beverage. This was the first and last time we ever spoke. He says to me, "What the fuck were you telling my brother the other night?" And I was like, "Your brother? Who's your brother?" We go back and forth a bit, and I realize all three of these dudes are related. They're all brothers. All three of them. So I say something dismissive, something along the lines of "I was just telling your brother that his sonic aesthetics latently promote inclusion and recognize intersectionality, and that he dexterously sees through the institutionalized facade that dictates musicians must play their own instruments and write their own material in order to galvanize relevancy." He seemed to dig what I was saying, but he didn't say much in response. He nodded, gave me my change, and jacked the volume back up. So I went home.

That's the whole story.

That's the extent of what I know.

You all seem to act like there's something obvious here I'm not telling you. If there is, it's not obvious to me. Sometimes two plus two equals five. The reason I always went in there was to get a can of Mountain Dew. Mountain Dew, to me, is delicious. It's the single-best beverage there is, and I can't understand people who don't love it. But you know what's wild? You know what I consider to be the single-*worst* beverage on earth? Diet Mountain Dew. You couldn't pay me to drink that dog piss. So you tell me: How is this possible? How can the relationship between two things that are supposed to be almost identical be so different? How can two things that are supposed to be interchangeable exist on opposite polarities? There's no answer, so why ask the question? It's the same thing with this incident. You're talking to the wrong guy about the wrong thing.

I saw the police tape when I tried to get in there Monday afternoon. And like I told the original woman for her original report, I have no clue how anyone could beat somebody to death with a portable stereo. This shit is above my pay grade. I wanted a twelve-ounce can of Mountain Dew. That's it. This is not my affair. But will you at least tell me who got killed? I think I deserve to know.

Pain Is a Concept by Which We Measure Our God

THE DOCTOR SITS BEHIND A DESK, SPEAKING TO A MAN AND A woman. The conversation is happening in a world that looks and feels identical to our own, with the same history and the same mechanics. But this world is not our world. This world is better.

They are discussing the Procedure.

"The question is not whether or not you should do this," the doctor says. "The question is mostly about whether or not your insurance covers the implant and how you want it to function. At this point, it's hard to justify *not* doing this, at least in some limited capacity, particularly if you have coverage for both the insertion and the removal. In the past, some plans only covered the front end, so the removal was out-of-pocket. But that's become less and less common, and it's actually not that expensive, anyway. I would check with your HR department, just to make sure."

"We're covered and we want to do it," said the woman. "I've been reading about this for a long time, way before I was pregnant. We both understand the technology, more or less. What we don't know is the normal way to do this. Like, how are most other people doing it?"

"That's a loaded question. There is no normal," said the doctor. He slid open the drawer of his desk and pulled out two spiked silver spheres, each one smaller than the head of pin. He held one between his thumb and index finger. "These are the most basic implants," he said. "We go in through the ear and plug it into the dorsal posterior insula. With adults, the process is easy. Fifteen minutes. Your dentist could probably do it. It's trickier on a newborn, but not by much. And once both individuals have the implant, it works almost instantly. You can't jump *all* the pain, but you can jump most of it. Ninety percent at an absolute minimum. The average transfer is around ninety-seven percent. Ninety-seven percent is a reasonable expectation."

"What happens to the other three percent?" the man asked.

"Pain, as your wife has probably read, isn't like someone pressing a button inside your brain," the doctor explained. "It's not that contained. It's not that isolated. Pain is a ghost. It bleeds into everything. So the source patient will still feel *something*. There's a sensation and some disorientation. The source patient ingests the extraneous three percent. Nothing that hurts, though."

The man had a second question he didn't know how to ask. He tried anyway.

"You know, I saw this British TV show on Netflix," he began. But the doctor cut him off.

"It's not like that," the doctor said. "I know what you're going to ask, and it's not like that at all. So many people have asked me that question that I finally went back and watched the show you're referring to, which I enjoyed. But this will be nothing like that. This is not a way to share pain. This is a way to move pain from one host to another. And the recipient won't feel the same *specific* pain the source generates. It's not like your wife will experience pain in her cervix and you'll experience the same level of pain in your penis. We distribute the pain evenly throughout your whole body, in order to mitigate the impact. For example, let's say you decide to do this for the birth only, which is what most people—"

"Yes," interrupted the woman. "Explain how that works."

"Of course," said the doctor. "Once you're full-term, we implant the transmitter into your insula. We generally don't implant the receptor into your partner until the labor starts, since it's logistically helpful for the woman to feel the onset of her contractions. Like I said, the insertion is a fifteen-minute procedure. We can do it in the ER if necessary. Once the receptor is secure and the connection is locked, the pain flows straight across the bow. Any sensation the source contextualizes as discomfort automatically migrates to the recipient, as long as they're on the same Wi-Fi network. No need for an epidural. No need for opiates. The mother will feel the fetus sliding through the birth canal, but that transition won't be remotely excruciating. One woman told me it felt like swallowing gelatin in reverse. The recipient, of course, will feel something quite different. The cliché is that it's like being tased from the inside out. Most partners choose to be sedated for the process. Some like to sit in a warm bath and drink beer or wine, which we allow. But we do require that the recipient remain conscious, for the safety of all involved parties."

"What could go wrong?" asked the man. "Why would it be unsafe for me to be unconscious?"

"He's just being cautious," said the woman. "He's just telling us what he has to tell us, because he's a doctor. This is not dangerous. Right? It's been widely reported that this procedure is not dangerous. Right? Nothing ever goes wrong."

"That's basically true," said the doctor. "There's never been a fatality or a successful malpractice lawsuit. There's always a minuscule possibility of circulatory shock. But even if that were to happen, it would be happening inside a hospital. It couldn't happen in a better place."

"We're doing this," said the woman. "We've made our decision."

"Excellent," said the doctor. "I will get the initial paperwork started and we can talk about the specifics in our next visit. Give me ten minutes to print and collate the copies. In the meantime, read this brochure and see if you have any questions before moving forward. Read the back page first, and pay special attention to the third point and the last point."

The doctor handed the couple a five-page pamphlet and left the room. The image on the front was a cartoon of two rabbits—one smiling and pregnant and one screaming and pulling its ears. The man grabbed the document from his wife's hands and immediately flipped it over.

NATAL PAIN MIGRATION:

SIX THINGS TO CONSIDER BEFORE YOU PROCEED

1. This is a shared responsibility. Do not agree to this exchange unless both parties are comfortable with the intensity of the experience.

2. Not all "pain" is *pain*. Migration is a technological process, but also an intellectual process. The transfer of sensation only occurs if the source actively perceives that sensation as negative and categorizes it within her own abstract definition of what constitutes "pain." If, for example, the source needs to urinate, the recipient will (probably) not feel that mild discomfort; if, however, the source chooses not to empty her bladder for four or five hours, the discomfort will (almost certainly) cross over to the recipient.

3. Pain is not gender specific. Most studies suggest that males have a higher tolerance for pain than females. This, however, does not apply to all couples. It is unwise to transfer negative feelings from a woman with a high threshold of pain into the body of a

partner whose threshold is significantly lower. Some men also feel an obligation to absorb their partner's discomfort due to social pressure. Keep in mind that this belief is antiquated.

4. This is a short-term, situational solution. It is not uncommon for couples—particularly following C-section evacuations or births requiring vaginal incisions—to request that the implants remain inside the cranium of both parties during the first few days of recovery. Though this decision is always left to the purview of the involved parties, it is strongly discouraged. The highest risk involved with this procedure is the possibility of the source patient injuring herself due to a lack of awareness (i.e., casually placing her hand on a hot stove or failing to recognize the symptoms of appendicitis). Pain exists for a reason. We advise removing the implants as soon as possible.

5. Infant implantation is not recommended. Many parents, upon the birth of their child, feel an overwhelming (and understandable) desire to place an implant inside the newborn's brain and absorb all discomfort from the vulnerable child's early maturation. This, while possible, is strongly discouraged, unless the newborn faces a medical threat that is terminal in nature.

6. Some pain is unknowable. The transfer of physical pain through this procedure is precise and objective. The transfer of emotional pain is not. If the individual giving birth experiences profound emotional distress (such as scenarios where the newborn is deformed or not responsive), the pain recipient may experience a high degree of unspecific menace. The residue of this exchange can sometimes be permanent, even following the removal of the implant. If this occurs, ask your physician to place you in contact with a therapist or psychologist specializing in this rare condition.

The office door opened and the doctor returned. He stepped behind the desk and pushed a stack of paperwork toward the couple, along with two pens. He joked that the process of transferring pain between two human bodies was only slightly less complicated than applying for a mortgage. The man was not amused.

"I'm not so sure about this," said the man. "This last point on the list—the thing about emotional pain that can last forever—that seems bad. Is it like PTSD or something? It never goes away?"

"It's extremely rare," said the doctor. "Extremely. And honestly, we haven't been doing this long enough to verify that it *never* goes away. It might, over time. It might fade. We only know that it can last after the implant is removed. But it's complicated. Since it only happens if the mother experiences a traumatic event, we don't know if her partner's symptoms are due to the transfer of the pain or a by-product of the event itself. I mean, God forbid, let's say there's an intrapartum death. Let's say, God forbid, that the child is stillborn. Your wife will comprehend that event intellectually, and a massive spike of existential despair will jump into your body. That's going to hit you like a ton of bricks. But then a nurse will take you aside and explain what actually happened, and that conversation will hit you just as hard. And then the implant will be removed from your wife's brain, and she will have to confront the emotional consequence of what has just happened for the first time, and you will have to help her through that. So the sense of doom that lingers with the recipient might be how any normal person would feel in the wake of any tragedy. We just don't know, and we can't know."

The man listened to this and felt better, although not much. The Procedure would be fine, probably. Nothing would happen, probably. He wanted to do this. It seemed like the right thing to do, and there was nothing worse than seeing his wife in pain. A few of his male coworkers had gone through the Procedure and bragged about it constantly. The technology was fascinating, and he viewed himself as the kind of person who adopted new ideas before they became standard. Yet something about the concept still worried him, even though he couldn't explain what it was. He and his wife had talked about this at length, always framed as a choice they both perceived as obvious. But now he was staring at the paperwork and holding a ballpoint pen, and he started to wonder if perhaps he had not thought about this decision with the depth it demanded.

"Can I ask a possibly dumb question," the woman said politely. "The fifth item on this list. I know it says you shouldn't—"

"I wish they wouldn't include that at all," the doctor interrupted. "It's on the list for the express purpose of telling people not to do something, and all it does is plant the seed. Here's the thing: It will be bad for your baby's development if you take away its pain. I realize it's always difficult when a baby is teething or has a fever or gets circumcised. It's hard to hear them cry when there's nothing you can do to help. You can only be as happy as your least happy child. But taking pain away from an infant always ends badly. I know of one couple in Tokyo who didn't remove the implant from their son's brain until he was almost two. That was over three years ago, and he's still having a hard time adjusting to reality. He can barely walk. Kids need pain in the same way they need milk. Kids need pain."

"But when does that stop?" asked the man, finally recognizing the core of his apprehension. "How do we know adults don't need pain? Isn't it possible that childbirth is supposed to be painful for the woman?"

"Why would that possibly be?" asked the doctor.

"Yes," said his wife. "Please explain why it's supposed to be normal for me to experience pain while you experience nothing."

"I don't know why. If I could answer the question I wouldn't need to ask it," said the man. "I'm not a doctor and I'm not a philosopher. I have no idea why this would be true, beyond the fact that this is how it's always been before. I realize that things change. But still. Why are we migrating the pain into another person? Why not put the reception implant into an animal? A pig. A monkey. Why not an elephant? An elephant would barely notice."

"Because that would be cruel," said the doctor.

"Okay, fine," the man continued. "Then how about a convicted murderer? How about some child rapist sitting in a supermax? How about war criminals? Why does it have to go into *me*? You could jump this pain anywhere, into anyone. I could probably pay some college kid to take it. Why do I have to absorb someone's agony just because I happen to love them?"

"Because we're married," said his wife. "Because that's what love is."

The papers were signed. The baby was perfect.

What About
the Children

WANT THE CLASSIC CULT SHIT," SAID EZRA, FINALLY EXPRESSING HIS central desire with a clarity we'd spend the next ten years suppressing. "We're not doing this to break new ground. I'm a traditionalist. There's no point in pursuing this if we don't adopt the classic style."

I'd love to say I tried to reason with him, but I didn't try at all. Our relationship wasn't like that. Even when I was twelve and he was four, I would always reinforce his worst tendencies. At the time, it seemed like I was supposed to do that. It seemed like it made me a good brother. And what can I say? His mischievous ideas amused me. He was such a charismatic autocrat. All his little friends in the neighborhood would do whatever he wanted. He would convince them to play kickball in the snow, while he drank hot cocoa and watched through the living room window.

"You think this is going to be so easy," said Taffy, perhaps the only person who ever aspired to be a wet blanket and just couldn't make it work. "This isn't the 1970s. Even Jonestown would have Google. You can't control people when they all have phones."

"We could take the phones away," I suggested. "That could be part of the attraction. We frame the whole thing as a neo-Luddite movement. We tell them to reject technology, for spiritual reasons."

"I considered that, but no," said Ezra. "For that to work, we'd need one hundred percent compliance, and that's impossible. It's too easy to get inside a public library. One malcontent jumps onto Reddit and the whole thing implodes. A better move is tacking in the opposite direction. We specifically target people *obsessed* with the Internet and convince them that the Internet will eventually cause the end of the world, which is what most people obsessed with the Internet already believe. We tell them that this technological apocalypse is our organizational goal, and that they've been chosen by God to help this happen. We tell them to spend all day online. We demand it. We tell them to pump out misinformation on purpose. After a while, they'll assume misinformation is the only information there is, and then the problem disappears."

What can I say? Counterintuitive logic was the only logic he understood.

Taffy, to her credit, was never fooled. She's only two years older than Ezra, so certain aspects of his personality I find charming do not work on her. I remember when she was going to be a junior at Carleton and Ezra decided he wasn't going to college at all, and our dad said, "You know, different people can be smart in different ways." I sometimes think that was the real reason she quit school. And then when she did, our dad was like, "Why, Taffy? Why would you do that? How will you survive?" Our father just had no sense of his own subtext. But then Taffy moved in with Ezra and never left, so maybe I misread the whole thing.

"You need to talk him out of this," Taffy told me. This was after it was already too late. "We're all going to end up in prison. In fact, prison might be the best-case scenario. He's such a cement head. He doesn't even know how to be successfully immoral."

"You don't have to be involved with this," I told her at the time. We were eating spaghetti and watching *Top Chef: All-Stars* in the back of my minivan. We did that sometimes. We loved eating in the car. "You're a huge asset, but you shouldn't feel obligated."

"He doesn't even realize that cults don't call themselves *cults*," said Taffy. "That's only what other people call cults, so that the cultists can deny it. How can someone not know that? He also doesn't seem to realize that a cult leader has to *sort of* believe whatever it is he's claiming. Rajneesh sort of believed his own bullshit. Koresh, certainly. Applewhite, certainly. Manson, probably. I suppose L. Ron Hubbard might be the exception that proves the rule, but that's not going to work twice."

"Maybe simplicity is his silver bullet," I told her. "He's cutting out the middleman."

"You need to talk him out of this," said Taffy. "You're the only person he listens to, and he doesn't even listen to you."

"Here again, I want to stress that you don't need to be involved with this. You really don't, Taff."

"I know," she said. "But at least if it's us, it can't be anyone else."

It was hopeless, and I knew it was hopeless, and I'm pretty sure I opened the conversation by saying, "This is probably hopeless." But Taffy wanted me to try, so I tried. I'll always do whatever Taffy wants. The three of us had spent the day strategizing, as usual, and just before Ezra left the loft (he always left early) I told him to meet me for dinner back at my house around seven. I fried up some haddock and waited for him on the porch. I could see him coming up the sidewalk from three blocks away. He was wearing a dashiki, which meant either he knew I was going to confront him (and was trying to throw me off my game) or, more likely, he was about to offer some inane, persuasive explanation as to why it made sense for an unemployed twenty-eight-year-old Caucasian to wear a West African wedding garment on a summer night in Duluth. I elected to pretend I didn't notice. There was no reason to be clever, so I jumped straight into the crux of the psychosis: He was working off a flawed model. I told him it wouldn't succeed, and that it might be worse if it did. I explained that these kinds of sects needed to start organically, and that people would not respond to a guru who did not give a shit about spirituality, and that people in northern Minnesota probably wouldn't respond to a guru even if they believed he was totally sincere. He listened, and he removed his sunglasses. That was almost a win. But he behaved like we were merely having another conversation about strategy.

"Don't worry. We're definitely relocating," said Ezra. "San Francisco is still ground zero for this kind of thing, both for the hippies and for the tech angle." This transitioned into a lecture about how California would also be better suited for the sexual component of the cult, as Ezra planned on impregnating all female members who were open to the concept. I stopped him cold and explained that this was precisely the kind of thinking that concerned Taffy and me. I told him he was preoccupied with the wrong things. He agreed, but only because he thought I was criticizing his unwillingness to focus on tax-exempt revenue streams. "I think our best option is money laundering," he said. "I mentioned this to Taffy, and she tried to talk me out of it. However, in the process of telling me why we shouldn't do it, she explained how money laundering actually works, which—as it turns out—I didn't fully understand. But now that I know, I'm certain it's what we should be doing. Money laundering is our kind of crime."

"Dammit, Ezra, this is why we're worried. You can't use words like *crime* in casual conversation. You can't run around saying, *Our cult is going to commit excellent crimes.* Hermetic societies can't be planned in advance."

"I appreciate your candor," said Ezra, "but I'm afraid I must beg to differ. You're still acting like this is an innovative idea. It's not. It's a regular idea. Look at it like a regular job. Everybody knows what's up. It's like the difference between the first season of *Survivor* and the last season of *The Bachelor*. We no longer need to sell people on the premise. Only on the details."

Ezra believed that people who joined cults were no longer marginalized radicals searching for a larger purpose, nor were they lost outcasts with low self-esteem and dysfunctional families, nor were they bookish slackers hungry for enforced structure or alternative spiritual pursuits. All that, he insisted, had ended with the twentieth century. Ezra believed that modern people who joined cults were simply people who already self-identified as the kind of person who might join a cult, and that they would prefer a cult that was unambiguous about its cultic tendencies. They would expect to be swindled. They would demand sexual deviancy and asinine nicknames. They would be disappointed if they were allowed to consume processed foodstuffs and wear non-monochromatic clothing. Every time I tried to counterpunch, he would use my own words against me, even if my words didn't apply to the new thing we were debating. What can I say? His bad faith had panache. By the time we were eating the fish, I'd begrudgingly accepted the banality of his evil. It was fun to listen to him talk. I admired his resolve. You know, an older brother can't really be jealous of a younger brother. That's the one thing *The Godfather* got wrong. But I did wonder what it would be like to have his level of conviction. I could never act the way he seemed to act all the time.

The move west happened about a year after the haddock supper. San Francisco was too expensive and Oakland wasn't much cheaper, so we ended up in San Jose (not ideal, but Ezra liked that it had once been home to an incestuous vampire coven). We rented a dilapidated Lutheran church and stopped paying rent after the first six months (eviction laws in California are fantastic). I oversaw member recruitment and day-to-day maintenance. Taffy handled the finances, the infrastructure, media relations, marketing, and the legal department. Ezra delivered a five-hour lecture three times a week, usually about the alleged technological rapture but also about his various pet interests (wind power, gerrymandering, symphorophilia, the music of Tool). The only significant conflict I can recall from those early days was a fracas over what we would call ourselves. Ezra wanted to name our organization the California Super Cult, which Taffy deemed legally suicidal and which I feared would be taken as irony (I get what he was going for, but it was too cute by half). We eventually convinced Ezra to compromise and replace the word *cult* with the word *family*, since that was almost as explicit to anyone who'd care. But (of course) he had to go further and call it the Last Family of Fire and Darkness, just to ensure no one made the mistake of thinking four hundred people wearing cobalt tracksuits and eating steel-cut oats in an abandoned church basement was some kind of Uber-sponsored disruption stunt.

What can I say? It was easier than I thought. Attracting members was not difficult. We just had to act trippy and make a big point of not blinking whenever we were in public. Ezra had been right about almost everything. The misinformation campaign worked perfectly and may have inadvertently rekindled the romance between Jerry Brown and Linda Ronstadt. New recruits happily emptied their savings accounts upon indoctrination, not to mention the unexpected windfalls we earned through online gambling and Bitcoin. Our drug-fueled orgies were epic and received a nice write-up from BuzzFeed. Ezra sired twenty-eight children, all of whom were named Ezra. Sometimes the conditions were tough on Taffy, as she regularly worked seventeen-hour days and never stopped being annoyed by church members' referring to her little brother as the Hydra Yahweh, which (in his defense) wasn't even Ezra's idea. Still, I could tell she enjoyed the responsibility, in her own quiet way. She liked the power and believed she deserved it. Ezra spent an increasing amount of every week in seclusion, so the compound was her own private Alcatraz. He came up with the rules, but she constructed the language and enforced every policy. She was great at it. We weren't causing any trouble, locally or spiritually. Our organized crimes were minor and undiscovered, and the only reason we committed them at all was to complete the cliché. We were happy people. There's nothing like working with your own family. It was a wonderful decade, up until today. But now I don't know what to think.

Like any other Monday, Taffy and I met with Ezra in his sleeping chamber to plan the week's schedule and outline any forthcoming manipulations of reality. This weekly meeting is often dull and always frustrating, but also a nice chance for the three of us to spend some time together. I always looked forward to it. Today, however, was different. Ezra seemed like his normal self, except he kept casually mentioning guns, and the acquisition of guns, and why we needed a larger gun budget, and the essentiality of gun stockpiling within the enduring cult paradigm. Taffy and I kind of rolled our eyes, familiar with Ezra's flights of fancy. But this was different. He just kept going. He started talking about types of poisons and the best way to control a fire. By the time he was theorizing about how the compound could be sealed from the inside and flooded with carbon monoxide, Taffy had lost her patience.

"I have a shitload of work to do, Ezra. Quit wasting our morning," she said. "Let's get back to the lunch menus."

"The menus don't matter," said Ezra. "It's been ten years. We've accomplished everything we intended. By any standard, we're an all-time top twenty cult. I'd stack our body of work against anyone. But we've all had enough. It's time to reset."

"What are you talking about?"

"What do you mean, what am I talking about? It's time for the suicides."

"Ezra," said Taffy, "I'm not going to pretend like this is interesting. Let's move on."

"Don't act like this is some kind of unexpected twist," said Ezra. "We've always known this was a suicide cult, from the very beginning. Do you really think I would have started a cult that *wasn't* a suicide cult? What would be the point of that?"

"This was never on the table," I said. "I'm not killing myself."

"Well, of course not," said Ezra. "Neither am I. Neither is Taffy. *We're* not going to die. Are you fucking crazy? The suicides are only for the others. Taffy can organize the methodology. We'll let the kids live, of course. We won't kill the little Ezras."

"So this is your brilliant vision," said Taffy. "This whole time, all this work. The endgame was—what? Force everyone to kill themselves, leave a bunch of orphans, and spend the rest of our lives as fugitives? For no reason."

"We'll go back to Duluth," said Ezra. "We'll start something different. Another family business. We're clearly a good team. I was thinking maybe a marijuana dispensary."

"You think they're just going to let us leave town?" asked Taffy, still unsure if she was actually having the conversation she was actually having. "You think they're going to find four hundred corpses in an old church basement and not wonder what happened? You think they won't want to maybe ask you what the fuck went down?"

"They'll think I'm dead," said Ezra. "I've been sending Retro Rodney to the dentist."

Retro Rodney was the nickname for Rodney Brewhouse. He'd been a member from the very beginning.

"You've been sending Rodney to the dentist," Taffy said flatly.

"I've been sending Rodney to the dentist *as me*. I told him it was part of the misinformation campaign. Every time he goes in, I tell him to demand that the dentist take some X-rays. So those are my dental records now. Once Rodney is dead, I'll drag him up here and burn off his face and cut off his hands and put my wallet in his tracksuit. His teeth will do the rest."

"Ezra," I said. "That's not cool. Rodney is a good dude."

"You know we have to do this," said Ezra. "Both of you. You both understand. You can't create a cult and then decide you're just going to become a commune. That's not how it works. I know you both love telling me that I don't understand how the world works, but now I'm telling you. This is a cult. It's a textbook cult. I'm a deranged cult leader. My actions can't be explained. We're going to tell all those morons to kill themselves, and they're going to do it. Don't worry about the little kids. The kids will be fine. It will be all over the news when they find the bodies, and some philanthropist will swoop in and adopt every Ezra. Who knows? It might even be Angelina Jolie or something. I'll be the villain, except to the kind of people who love reading books about cult leaders. They'll just think I'm complicated."

"Why do you always do this?" asked Taffy. "Why do you always ruin my shit?"

"I'm not ruining any shit. I'm only doing what we all agreed to do," said Ezra. "Now go plan our genocide and give me a chance to nap. The meeting is adjourned."

What can I say? I love my brother. I want him to succeed. There's nobody else like him. His enthusiasm is contagious. He goes for the jugular. But Taffy is going to the police, and she says I have to go with her, and I always do what Taffy wants. Her contention is that Ezra wants to watch people die as proof of their misplaced loyalty in a persona he created for his own arbitrary amusement. My counter is that, even though that's probably true, he could never get it together enough to actually impose the suicides unless we helped him. Ezra lives in a bubble. He has no idea what stores even sell poison. It seems like we could just stall for time and he'd eventually move on to something else. Six months from now, I could see him scrapping the whole suicide plan and trying to start a goat farm instead. But Taffy thinks otherwise, and I have to trust her on this. Different people can be smart in different ways, but not really.

Taffy says we probably won't even go to jail for that long. There will be a tax evasion issue, there will be a bunch of minor racketeering charges, and maybe an accusation of fraud. But we're not getting raided, so she can burn all the paperwork and I can clear the hard drives. The members don't know anything about the theoretical suicides and are still psychologically on our side. They won't want to testify. They'll say whatever we tell them to say. Ezra might get six years, at the most. Taffy and I should be out in eighteen months. I'm not looking forward to jail, but it's not the end of the world. One underrated upside to living in a cult is that life inside a prison isn't that different.

That said, it really bums me out. Our parents would be disappointed. I always felt like they trusted me to make sure Taffy and Ezra understood that their relationship had to be unconditional. They both had so much potential, which I never had, outside of my aptitude for getting along with people who are hard to get along with. That was big for my mom. I remember eavesdropping on one of her telephone conversations, and she was telling the woman on the other end of the line, "It would be so easy if all the kids were like Thad. Everybody likes him. He always sees the good in everybody." That made me feel so goddamn happy. But now I have to ruin Ezra's life, and Ezra is going to hate Taffy forever, and nobody will blame me, but I know it's my fault.

(An Excerpt from)

A Life That Wasn't Mine

AUTUMN WAS IDENTICAL TO SUMMER, JUST AS SUMMER HAD BEEN indistinguishable from spring. The Santa Ana winds ripped catawampus across the 405 as we drove to work, a twenty-two-minute trip that sometimes took two hours. Sarah studied her phone in the passenger seat while politically aware rap music we both pretended to understand pummeled us from the Audi's factory speakers. These were good times for us. We were finally working at the same studio, so this commute had become the crux of our marriage. Sarah had shoehorned her way into a job well suited for her skill set: She was responsible for excavating the oceanic floor of unexploited action-comedy scripts from the 1980s and repurposing them for use in the present day, a task primarily requiring her to manufacture scenarios where a character either (a) lost his cell phone or (b) inexplicably forgot to replenish its battery. It was as repetitive as it was essential, since pretty much every fictional crisis conceived during the Reagan administration could have been averted if the protagonist had access to a mobile phone. This was all Sarah did, all day. Her crowning achievement was a retooling of a lost Shane Black script later transformed into the sleeper hit *Boom Time*. In the original 1985 screenplay, the heroine misreads a street sign on her way to a dinner party and mistakenly enters an abandoned warehouse filled with C-4 plastic explosive and rapist ninjas. Sarah circumvented the problem by making the character a devout Orthodox Jew, scheduling the fictional dinner party on a Shabbat Saturday, and deleting most of the rapes. She was also lauded for her edit on the profitable remake of *Home Alone*, a narrative resuscitated by her addition of a subplot involving a black bear that enters the family residence and eats all the phone chargers.

My job was less creative, albeit more lucrative. I'd been promoted into a leadership role within the Life Rights Division, a high-stress, low-profile, mid-prestige management position. Life rights (which I assume almost any reader of this memoir already understands) involve the legal acquisition of a given individual's life story for use in film or television. The process isn't necessary if the subject of the film is already dead, and—technically—you don't need to own someone's life rights in order to insert them into a movie, assuming they're a public figure. But it always helps. By purchasing a person's life rights, you're essentially purchasing the individual's full cooperation with the project. You're also protected from the risk of a defamation suit, if you accidentally or intentionally denigrate the person in question. Which, I cannot deny, was almost always the studio's unspoken objective.

I was good at my job. I was competent and dependable, and I had one immediate success, unexpectedly acquiring the life rights to novelist Jonathan Franzen (the box-office failure of the subsequent biopic, *Typewriter Birdwatcher*, was not held against me). But that acquisition was something of an anomaly. The vast majority of my work involved non-celebrities whose lives nonetheless warranted potential transfer to the silver screen: a coal miner who had been trapped in a hot air balloon, a blind Alabama neurosurgeon, a suburban mother who'd purchased a Chewbacca mask at Kohl's. On slow days, I'd search for teenagers with unusually large Instagram followings and acquire their life rights in perpetuity, usually for less than $7,500. Why not? It was like buying pull-tabs. Low risk, high reward. But then, as is so often the case in this knife-fucking Astroturf shittown, everything I'd built collapsed into sulfur. And that was entirely due to *Untitled Nessie Project*.

Had the studio followed the initial high-concept vision for *Untitled Nessie Project*, my involvement would have been completely unnecessary: The original script was about the Loch Ness Monster attacking tourists. That was the whole story. The script was then redrafted so that the monster was saving tourists, and then rewritten a third time, with the monster now saving tourists from a shore-dwelling Sasquatch. It was not expected to be a theatrical release. Syfy seemed like a best-case scenario. But then something preposterous occurred: *Untitled Nessie Project* was inadvertently messengered to the office of *Inception* director Christopher Nolan, who left it in the car of his brother (*Westworld* creator Jonathan Nolan), who loaned that car to his twenty-two-year-old personal assistant, a woman who happened to go on a series of dates with a then twenty-nine-year-old Parker Troglovich. Now, I realize Troglovich has become something of a dark joke in the industry, and justifiably so—he treated people horribly, his final three films were abysmal, and his death was both suspicious and formulaic. But at that particular moment in time, he was the hottest director in the hemisphere. Critics had loved his unsentimental debut *Dead Antelope*, and it had become trendy to suggest his sophomore effort, *Kiki Vandeweghe*, should have won the Oscar for Best Picture. His power was unlimited, at least temporarily. So when "Trog" (as we all called him) discovered a script on the floorboard of a car he was using for oral sex, there was no doubt that script would become a major motion picture. Every light he encountered would glow neon green.

But Trog, of course, had ideas.

Trog was impossible to work with. It was a reputation he cultivated. While shooting *Kiki*, he made the entire cast transcribe recipes from out-of-print East German cookbooks in between takes, never explaining the purpose for doing so. An outspoken vegan, he did not allow the presence of leather on any filming location, except for his own pants (which he never washed). He allegedly lied to a well-respected character actress minutes before shooting a scene, claiming that her father had just been hospitalized with a stroke, solely to get the desired performance (which, somewhat paradoxically, was framed as comedic). He was hyperkinetically capricious, once firing and rehiring the same key grip three times in a single morning, despite the fact that it was Easter Sunday and the whole crew was on holiday. But mostly he was stubborn, particularly about his conception for what *Untitled Nessie Project* was supposed to be. For the entirety of the ill-fated production, up until the very day the money was gone and the plug was pulled, he repeatedly voiced the same refrain: "The beast is an illusion." Which was his way of explaining why this Loch Ness Monster movie would not involve the Loch Ness Monster in any context whatsoever.

How (or why) Trog arrived at this actuality remains opaque. In the script found in the car, the monster appears on-screen in nineteen of the fifty-four outlined scenes. Trog went in a different direction. "The monster will be present," he explained to the cast, "but not literally." The word *monster* was deleted entirely and the dialogue never referenced any kind of aquatic creature. The monster would not be represented visually. The monster would not be used as a metaphor and the monster would not be used as a MacGuffin. Yet we would still shoot on location in Scotland, with 3-D cameras (an equally perplexing decision, as this would now be a costume drama). The film would be set on the shores of Loch Ness in 1972, in and around a palatial manor once owned by occultist Aleister

Crowley that had been purchased by Led Zeppelin guitarist Jimmy Page. This residence, locally referred to as Boleskine House, overlooked the loch from the adjacent Scottish Highlands. The bulk of Trog's reimagined screenplay fixated on a heroin-addicted Page, sitting on the floor of a dank room in the lotus position, attempting to conjure Crowley's spirit in hopes of using mind bullets to murder Keith Richards of the Rolling Stones. The story was now told from the perspective of a nosy neighbor with a biracial love interest. A decomposing woodchuck played a key narrative role. The new script was only eleven pages long, but projected to transmute into a 150-minute movie. I recall numerous dream sequences and one seamless stedicam shot of the Page character wordlessly skulking about his residence for more than nine minutes, set against the seventeenth-century composition "Sonata per Chitarra, Violino e Basso Continuo," an Italian classical piece some believe to be the sonic inspiration for "Stairway to Heaven." Further complicating matters was the realization that Boleskine House had burned to the ground in 2015, prompting Trog to demand a full-scale replica be rebuilt from scratch over the remnants of the ashes and rubble. I was first introduced to Trog two weeks into pre-production. The project was already twenty months behind schedule.

My appointed mission in all this was, seemingly, quite simple. There was no way the location of the film could be changed, since there is only one lake widely known for housing a mythical creature (the fact that there was no monster in the script did not matter, as Trog insisted the monster was still "the essential cog"). We could not create a fictional, composite rock musician to take the place of Jimmy Page, as he is the only rock musician who ever purchased a haunted mansion on the shores of Loch Ness; any unspecific composite character would still be viewed as Page himself, regardless of the character's appearance or behavior. Page was a public figure, so we could have made the picture without his consent or

assistance. However, the script was exceedingly false and deeply defama-
tory, and we almost certainly would have been hammered for a variety of
justifiable reasons (one of which being that Page and Richards were pretty
good friends). For this movie to succeed, I had to procure Jimmy Page's
life rights. It was the only way to make this work. Knowing nothing about
him (or his music), I was surprised by how many people told me this might
be challenging. These skeptics proved correct. I reached out to him twenty-
five times. His representatives declined the first three offers and ignored
the following twenty-two. I flew to London and knocked on the door of
his home in Kensington, unannounced. I was informed that I needed to
schedule a meeting, and that the meeting could not take place for four
days. I sat in my hotel room, watching the rain and the BBC. Just before
I was about to take a taxi back to his residence, I was couriered a polite
note from Page, which I still have in my archives. The letter stated that
he was not remotely interested in the film and would use all his resources
to legally stop its release. The rejection was followed by an additional
three handwritten pages detailing the data storage capability of pre-
WWII German magnetic tape and the sublime dynamic range of the
Telefunken 251 microphone.

I returned to Los Angeles to explain this to Troglovich (now recast-
ing the film for a third time, having decided to make the Page character
transgender). At first, he appeared to ignore me, almost as if the news I'd
just delivered would have no impact on the production. He declined to
read Page's note, except for the section about the microphone. The following Sunday, he showed up at my house in Silver Lake, stood on my porch,
and pedantically explained how I needed to lock down the Page life rights
within the next forty-eight hours. I told him I'd already invested months
working on nothing else, and that he needed to either move in a different
direction or make the film against Page's wishes and risk the lawsuit. He

did not agree, even though I'd said nothing that could be logically disagreed with.

"Page will comply," said Trog. "If he refuses to grant us his life rights, we will take them by force. Do what thou wilt."

Unsure how to respond, I asked what this meant.

"Who is to say who owns a life?" Trog asked rhetorically. For a man so small in stature, intimidation came easy. "The whole concept of life rights is a sad joke, and you are the sad jester who makes it. A person's story belongs to whoever has the testicles to make that story exist. I will take Page's life. I will take it! I will use it for my own creative purpose, which is the highest purpose there is. We all share the same reality. Correct? And if we all share the same reality, all lives are connected within that reality. Correct? Which means all lives are possessed collectively. He can't sell me his life rights, because he does not own them. No one does. They are available to everyone."

I explained that this is not how the law operates.

"Let me ask you something," he said. "Do you own the rights to your life?"

"Of course," I said.

"You do not," said Trog. "That's something you must learn."

He stepped off my porch, slid into his silver Pagani Zonda, and sped away. I explained the conversation to Sarah, and we both spent the night drinking ouzo and chuckling over Trog's petulance and absurdity. We laughed less when we showed up for work on Monday and realized that my parking space had been reassigned and our keys no longer opened the door.

Not That Kind
of Person

SHEILA KNEW SHE WANTED TO MURDER HER HUSBAND. THAT WASN'T the issue. The issue was that she had no idea how to make that happen. She knew she wasn't a killer. She didn't even use glue traps. She purchased an old trade paperback online, an anthology titled *The Mammoth Book of Killer Women*, hoping it might point her in the right direction. But all it did was remind her that most female murderers kill their victims with poison, and there was no way she was doing that. She would never kill someone with food. That would be an ideological affront to her career. Seeing no better option, she decided to hire a hit man, which was much harder than finding a used book on Amazon. She had to download Tor software. But nevertheless, she persisted, and it wasn't long before she was communicating with a wide variety of regional murderers-for-hire. Each potential killer made a viable pitch. A few employed emojis, most notably the emoji for "bullet." However, one candidate offered more than meat-and-potatoes murder. The man billed himself as the Ultimate Assassin, which Sheila initially found arrogant and a little on-the-nose. But the man insisted he could prove this moniker was no exaggeration. He offered to meet Sheila at her bakery to explain his methodology. He was persuasive, and his emails were grammatically correct. That was huge. There was no way Sheila would let someone execute her husband if the executioner didn't understand the difference between *your* and *you're*.

The meeting was set for ten in the morning. As a safety precaution, Sheila wanted to make sure they met when the bakery was crowded. But the moment the assassin stepped through the door, she realized there was no need for worry. He was congenial, well dressed, and passive. Tall, but never looming. Expensive haircut, fashion-forward eyeglasses, grown-up leather shoes. They shook hands and sat by a window. He asked several questions about the bakery and made a few insightful comments about the functional difference between a cake and a pie. He asked if she wanted to talk about money at the beginning of the conversation or at the end. Sheila said the end.

"How did you get into this line of work?" she asked. The assassin noted this was a common question.

Like most professional killers, he'd started in the military before entering the private sector. He'd been part of a death squad that usually worked in Central America and Eastern Europe, the kind of assignment members of the media always classified as black ops (though he chuckled at the reference and said no member of a real death squad would ever use a term so melodramatic). He didn't want to explain how he'd been recruited for this vocation, beyond saying he'd "received high scores" on tests that "reward pragmatism and violence." He said he'd only had direct involvement with three military assassinations in a span of eight years, but that the training exercises were challenging and informative and the ideal preparation for a life in private practice. He nonchalantly outlined the various ways to murder people and the pros and cons of each prospect. A "rando" was a one-man job committed in public, with the downside being a high possibility of failure. A "crash and bash" was a two-man job where a residence was forcibly entered and the scene was fixed to resemble a drug deal gone awry. A "fiver" required five attackers, with the goal of making the victim disappear without a trace. There were ways to make a homicide seem like an accident. There were ways to make it seem like the victim was actually the aggressor. There were ways to frame other people for the crime, but he said he didn't like to do that if it wasn't necessary (and if she did intend to frame someone for the murder, the price would be double). "There are obviously many ways to kill a husband," he said, "although I've developed my own style, which is the style I prefer."

Sheila listened to these details, enthralled and delighted. She was immediately convinced she'd selected the right applicant. She loved his approach to storytelling. "Do you want to know *why* I want to kill my husband?" she asked, assuming he'd say something cool and detached like, "That's never my concern." But his reaction was the opposite of her expectation. "Yes. Tell me everything," he said. "Is it okay if I take notes?"

Though she'd thought about this decision for months, Sheila had never spoken of it aloud and relished the opportunity to finally do so. Her husband was lazy, she said, and he was a liar. What's worse than a lazy liar? Nothing. He would say he was working late, but then he'd go to the bar, and when she caught him at the bar he'd try to claim he was actually there for work, but when she asked why he was working at the bar he would pretend like he was hurt that she didn't trust him, even though he was never genuinely hurt by anything. He would say they didn't have enough money to take a vacation, but then he'd buy a massive TV and claim he got it on sale, but then she'd call the store and it wasn't on sale at all. One summer, she thought he was having an affair, which she accused him of constantly. He said, "You know, if you keep accusing me of having an affair, I probably *will* have an affair, since that's what you seem to believe, anyway." That was two years ago. And since she'd never stopped making the accusation, the affair must have happened by now, unless he was lying about his intentions or his willingness to try, in which case he was still (at best) a lazy liar. Also, she did not love him and he did not love her, but he wouldn't get a divorce because he was Catholic and believed the virtuous move was to just spend the rest of their lives in misery.

"I see," said the assassin. "Your case is classic. Almost generic. I can absolutely work with this data. Now, before we go any further, we need to talk about the time frame. When do you want this to happen?"

"Soon," said Sheila. "Now. Today. Yesterday, if that were possible."

The man whistled. "I was afraid you might say that. That's a problem. That would require a more brutal approach, which is not my preference. To do it my way, I will need more time."

"How much more?"

"I'd estimate four years."

"Four years? I don't want to wait four years," said Sheila. "What kind of assassin takes four years to assassinate someone?"

"The ultimate assassin," said the Ultimate Assassin. "There's a reason I'm the best at this. I'm not like the other goons. Could I just walk up and blast your husband in the skull with a three-fifty-seven Magnum? Sure. That's one way to kill someone. But it's a stupid way to kill someone. That generates more problems than it solves. My preferred style is considerably more sophisticated. My style is the ultimate style."

"What does that even mean?"

"It means I will convince your husband to murder himself."

For the first time in her life, Sheila understood the sensation of buyer's remorse. She'd always known what that term meant, but she'd never felt it. It hit her in the face like a frying pan, even though she still hadn't paid this man a nickel.

"That's ridiculous," said Sheila. "I don't even know what that means or how it would work."

"I think you know exactly what it means, and how it works is my concern. This isn't like hiring a plumber. Every murder has problems. No murder is unsolvable. In the fifties, the CIA used to throw guys out of windows and blame it on LSD. That barely worked then and would never work now. There are always questions. There's always residue. If you kill this man, if I kill this man, if anyone kills this man—it won't be clean. Mistakes will be made, always. There will always be a few details that can't be explained, and people can end up in jail, and one of those people might be you. But not if this man kills himself. If he kills himself voluntarily, there is no killer to indict. The only perfect homicide is a legitimate suicide."

Sheila explained that her husband was the kind of guy who watched *It's a Wonderful Life* every December and cried during the closing credits. He was the kind of guy who ordered seafood in Omaha and rooted for the Cleveland Browns. He would never commit suicide.

"Of course he wouldn't. Not today," said the assassin. "That's why I need four years. I first need to manufacture a scenario where I meet your husband by chance and convince him to become my friend. That's the easy part. I slowly gain his trust. That's the hard part. I become his best friend, or at least his closest day-to-day confidant. That takes at least a year, maybe two. From there, I convince him that his life is terrible, which shouldn't be too difficult, if what you've told me is true. His marriage is bad, he's oppressed by religious ideology, he cares too much about TV. Who knows? He might be miserable already. And that's when we make our move. We pivot away from the limited view that *his* life is bad and toward the wider view that *life itself* is bad. That there is no hope for improvement, and that it wouldn't matter if there were. I leave a few books around his house—a little Plath, a little Camus. He won't even need to read them. He just needs to Google the authors' names out of curiosity. The net impact is identical. Maybe I invite him to my summer house on a rainy weekend and maybe we listen to Morrissey for two days. Maybe we have deep conversations about the hopelessness of existence. I ask rhetorical questions. I express admiration for authenticity and grit, and for men who follow through on difficult commitments. We drink red wine and stare at birds. And then, one day, it just happens. You come home, and there he will be, in the garage. The problem has solved itself."

The assassin leaned back in his chair and asked if he could sample a glazed doughnut.

"That's sick," said Sheila. "That's diabolical, not to mention implausible. There is no way I'm doing this. Get out of my bakery. Please. Get out of my bakery."

The assassin leaned forward.

"I apologize," he said. "I misread the seriousness of your request. If you want me to leave, I will leave. The customer is always right. But remember why I came here. You wanted me to kill your husband. Judging from what you said earlier, you wanted me to walk into your home and put a bullet in his brain. I'm offering a better solution. I'm offering the same service, but conducted humanely. The victim will have control over his final act. You will get what you want, and—in a way—so will he. In the end, he will welcome his own murder."

"You don't understand what I want," said Sheila. Did she want her husband dead? Of course she did. But she didn't want to make him depressed. She was not that kind of person.

Rhinoceros

LET ME PREFACE ALL THIS BY POINTING OUT SOMETHING THAT ISN'T important to anyone except me. I wasn't even reading the magazine. I don't read local magazines, particularly not local magazines that present themselves as national publications. It was a woman sitting next to me in the waiting room, waiting for her husband. She was the one who was reading the magazine. I was pretending not to look at her when I pretended not to see the photo on the opposite side of the page she was perusing. It was a photograph of Marvin, a familiar face I hadn't seen in years. He was not smiling. He had his arm wrapped around the waist of a cherry-haired woman who was also not smiling and who was also not his wife. I wouldn't describe my reaction as shock, but I was shook, which is only one letter away. I could immediately think of at least five reasons why this photo should not have existed. But then the receptionist called my name, and I had to walk away from a photo that shouldn't have existed in order to spend two hours lying on my stomach with a camera up my ass. When the procedure was over, I dragged myself back into the waiting area and found the discarded magazine on the floor. I decided to roll it up and take it with me. The upside to this decision was that I would not have to waste $5.99 on a local magazine. The downside was that I was now a thief who had to act casual as I limped out of the doctor's office. It also meant I couldn't open the magazine until I reached street level, so I had ninety additional seconds to consider why this photo was so disturbing.

Marvin was my closest friend among the many friends I no longer had any relationship with. He was widely considered the finest non-famous jazz writer in America, although I don't think he'd written about jazz in almost ten years, although I wasn't totally sure about that, since I'd never read an article about jazz in my entire life. He lived across the country with his wife and their two twin sons, both of whom were al-legedly math prodigies. I assumed the marriage was solid. He'd once sent me a digital Christmas card where the entire family was laughing and eating saltine crackers, a concept that felt too weird to be staged. He was notoriously private, having refused to grant even one interview for the release of his critically lauded, commercially unsuccessful book *How Not to Care About Things That Aren't Jazz*. Why would a local magazine in New York publish a story about an introverted jazz critic living in Seattle? Who was this provocative redhead I'd never seen before, and why was he touching her in such an intimate way? Why wasn't she smiling? Why wasn't he smiling? How did I not know what was going on with a person who would have likely been the best man in my wedding, had my fiancée not committed suicide days before the ceremony? It would have been a lot to process even if my rectum felt terrific.

I finally read the article on the K train, sitting on a pillow. It was like reading about someone I'd never met. There was only one dismis-sive sentence about Marvin's career as a jazz writer, halfway implying he now hated the entire genre. Marvin's wife, Donna, was never mentioned.

Most of the story's quotes were attributed to the red-haired woman from the photo, a self-described leftist propagandist who called herself Reckless Opportunist. Marvin still referred to himself as Marvin, although he lied about his age and made an awkward joke about how he would murder the president if he knew who the president was. The article didn't directly state that the pair was romantically conjoined, but the writer suggested as much in three separate paragraphs. The crux of the story was that Marvin and his female friend had figured out a way to delete Wikipedia entries with an embedded code that made it technologically impossible to replace the content that had been removed (it had something to do with an algorithm that operated as a retrovirus, but all the technical details were summarized in a sidebar I only skimmed). This, as it turns out, was a marginally illegal act. I wasn't aware it was illegal until I read the article, but I suppose the law makes sense: The legislation had been drafted around the same time Wikipedia merged with the public school system, back when there was justifiable fear over the notion of tampering with the official social record. The story in the magazine portrayed Marvin and his companion as counterculture heroes, encamped in a clandestine downtown apartment above an unnamed secret bar, intrepidly eliminating entries that deserved to be eliminated. Both Marvin and his accomplice were reticent to specify which subjects had already been purged, as doing so would contradict their larger intention. But they admitted the overall number of deletions was approaching two thousand, and Reckless was willing to confirm at least three—the entry for Robert E. Lee, the entry for Margaret Sanger, and the entry for Smashing Pumpkins.

To say this confused me would be akin to saying I enjoy mashed potatoes. I knew Marvin had become politicized after the 2004 election and I'd heard (through Facebook) that he'd been further radicalized by the Mossad assassination of Justin Trudeau. But this Wikipedia news was virgin chernozem. This was a complete reinvention, punctuated by an uncharacteristic embrace of insouciant cybercrime. Did something tragic happen to Donna? Social media indicated she was still in Seattle with the two boys, though her selected relationship status now read "nontraditional." I considered texting her, but we'd never texted previously. There was no thread to restart. We'd never had a sincere conversation since the weekend of the wedding and I didn't feel like pretending to care about how she was doing. I only wanted data. The lone mutual friend I could imagine being remotely helpful was my old racquetball partner Jacoby Foxcat, whom Marvin had lived with in the late nineties. I called him that night and asked if he knew what was going on with Marvin. Foxcat said, "Of course." But as we spoke, I realized he was just regurgitating the same information he'd gleaned from the same magazine I'd stolen from the ass doctor. He had no firsthand knowledge of anything. Foxcat hadn't interacted with Marvin since the finale of *Lost*. He was as confounded as I was, though much less interested in how or why this evolution had occurred. Jacoby assumed Marvin was just trying to make it seem like his midlife crisis wasn't cliché. He told me to relax and mind my own business. In the end, I regretted calling him at all.

A month passed. I had to go back uptown to the ass doctor for a follow-up visit. They always make you do that. I walk into the waiting room and almost soil myself: There sits Marvin, alone in the corner, reading an issue of *Grit*. He recognizes me instantly and seems happy, although not quite as happy as you're supposed to act when you unexpectedly encounter a long-lost friend. I ask him what he's doing in the office of my physician, and he says there's only one reason men our age see this kind of doctor. We both laugh. It's less uncomfortable than I would have guessed. I mention how I recently spoke to Jacoby Foxcat, and we spend a few minutes mocking his ineptitude as a racquetball player. I mention the magazine article, and Marvin acts slightly embarrassed and slightly proud. I sympathetically inquire about what went down with Donna, insinuating that I will take his side regardless of the answer. He tells me he met someone new who made him realize that he and Donna had never been in love. The bluntness of his description reminds me that Marvin is the kind of person who doesn't require niceties, so I directly ask him why he's illegally deleting Wikipedia entries. He says it's a hard thing to explain in public and that I should instead meet him and his new "lover" (his word) at their apartment tomorrow evening.

"I'd love for you to meet Reckless," he said. "She's an amazing cook. I'll tell her to whip up some mashed potatoes."

"Where do you two live?"

"There's a bar on the corner of Rivington and Essex called the Vagician," said Marvin. "Go up the back stairs after ten o'clock and knock five times on the red door. That's the code, if five knocks can count as a code. The doorman will let you into the upstairs bar. It's themed after the Soviet Union. The drinks are free. The bar is called Occupy Moscow."

"I don't get it," I say. "Aren't we supposed to put the word *occupy* in front of places that represent the tyranny of capitalism? Seems like Soviet-era Moscow would represent the opposite of that."

"Yeah, they didn't think that one through," said Marvin. "But behind the bartender, you'll see a rope ladder under a trapdoor. It looks sketchy, but it's safe. Climb up the ladder and open the trapdoor on the ceiling. That's our place. That's the place they gave us."

The receptionist called out a name I was unfamiliar with and Marvin got up and went to the front desk. It seemed pretentious to employ an alias at the proctologist, but I let it slide. He waved goodbye and said something about seeing me tomorrow at ten-thirty, and I responded affirmatively, like an idiot, almost by reflex. The idea of going somewhere I'd never been to meet a woman I'd never met and converse with a person I no longer knew was not appealing. I only wanted to know what was happening. I didn't want be *involved* with what was happening, regardless of what it was. But you know, I was curious, and it looked like this was the only way to get the information I wanted, and I'd already said yes (like an idiot). I had to go.

I consider wearing a suit, until I remember I'll evidently need to climb a rope ladder, prompting me to reverse polarity and go with sweatpants. The trains are fast and I arrive at the Vagician early. I'm able to finish two beers before heading up the staircase at 10:01. I knock five times on the red door and I'm instantly granted access. It's a dark bar with low ceilings and terrible music from the 1940s. There are at least a dozen nonconformists sitting around hardwood tables, drinking vodka and talking louder than necessary. The size of the crowd is perplexing, because I didn't see anyone else go up the back stairs before me. Is there a separate entry for regulars, or have they all been drinking up here for hours? To my surprise, I recognize someone in the corner of the room—a stocky, satirical novelist who often writes about oligarchs. He's telling an elaborate anecdote to three young Jewish women enraptured by his raconteuring. A man behind the bar robotically offers me a shot glass of vodka, but I wave him off and point toward the nine-foot rope ladder located behind him. He nods politely and allows me to pass. Up I go. It's been a long time since I touched a rope.

Before I even reach the trapdoor, I hear them arguing through the plywood. Marvin still fights the way I remember, a combination of deft sarcasm and muted exasperation. His red-haired roommate is straight-up screaming obscenities. The nature of the dispute is unclear, though my natural inclination is to worry that it somehow concerns my visit. I wait at the top of the ladder for almost two minutes, afraid to knock but acutely aware of the various Communists staring at my posterior. I finally rap on the bottom of the entrance, delicately. It opens in a flash. Marvin looks down and says, "You're early." But he instantly recognizes his rudeness and apologizes. He feigns excitement over my arrival while helping me into the loft. He introduces me to Reckless Opportunist. She is not dressed appropriately. I make sure to keep my line of vision above her neck.

"It's so nice to meet you," she says unconvincingly. "I hear you love mashed potatoes."

"My reputation precedes me," I say.

"I'm still cooking," she says. "It will be a while. You two can talk, or whatever it is you like to do."

She walks past both of us with her head down, disappearing into a different room that must be the kitchen but looks more like a bedroom. The apartment appears to have been decorated by a teenage boy with newly dead parents. Every wall is painted a different shade of orange. The smell of marijuana is suffocating. There are open laptops on the floor in every corner, surrounded by reference books. The only furniture is a massive collection of high-end beanbag chairs. We sit on the floor and try to make small talk, but Marvin is so visibly distraught that I admit I overheard the argument on my way up the ladder. I tell him I'll quietly leave if it's a bad time for a visit. Marvin, relieved that I've addressed the rhino in the room, assures me that the dispute is a minor dustup and that he and Reckless have a conflict-driven relationship, partly because of who they are and partly because of what they do. Seeing an opening to learn what I want to know, I ask him to elucidate.

"The magazine article explained it better than I could," said Marvin. "There are things in this world that don't need to be remembered. It's as simple as that."

"That doesn't seem simple at all," I say. "I don't understand how you would select what doesn't need to be remembered, and I don't understand how this magic algorithm keeps other people from just replacing whatever you eliminate."

"I don't understand the algorithm myself. That was all Toby," says Marvin. Toby is one of Marvin's teenage twins. "Toby is a genius. Tommy, not so much. He's a little overrated. I mean, don't get me wrong. Tommy's great. I love him. He gets all A's, he's solid in math. But Toby—that kid is a machine. He's described this algorithm to me ten different times and I still don't get how it works. It's almost like the shit deletes itself."

"But what is the purpose?" I ask. "It's not like eliminating the memory of an event changes what happened."

"I don't think you believe that," says Marvin. "If that was what you believed, you wouldn't think what we were doing was worth asking about. You wouldn't care at all. But you do care, because you know what we're doing is not insignificant. Concern over the elimination of any memory is proof that the memory itself has power. You should really ask Reckless to describe this in detail. I've thought about this stuff a lot, but she doesn't think about anything else."

"Is her name actually Reckless Opportunist?"

"Of course not. It's Courtney."

"How did the two of you meet?"

"She was Toby's tutor," said Marvin. "Toby wants to graduate at sixteen, so we needed to pump up his scores in the humanities. This was when he was still eleven or twelve. Reckless—this is back when she was still Courtney—worked for this private tutoring company that helps rich kids get into the Ivies. She would come over to the house three times a week, and I would eavesdrop on their sessions. And I just knew immediately. I knew I was in love with her, way before we ever made real contact.

The passion of her morality. The intensity of her hatreds. I just knew this was the woman I was supposed to be with. I couldn't control myself. I had to pursue her."

"How did Donna handle all this?" I ask. "How did you explain this to the boys?"

"The boys get it. They know who she is and they can see what she looks like. They understand what matters," said Marvin. "Donna wasn't thrilled, as you might expect. There was some crying, there was yelling. She threw a loaf of bread at me. She hit me with a tennis racket. But she's also not politically engaged, so there was almost no point in trying to explain."

"It seems like such a bold move," I say. "You just walked away from your family? You gave up on jazz?"

"No more jazz," said Marvin. "Say, do you want a tour of the apartment?"

"No," I replied. And I didn't. Why waste time with politeness? It wasn't like we were going to rekindle our friendship. I didn't recognize the person in front of me and I had no desire to pursue a fresh relationship with a new person who simply happened to resemble the old person I'd already lost touch with once before. But I did have more questions. I had so many questions that I didn't know where to start. How could Marvin blow up his entire life to be with a melodramatic woman who, while certainly sexy, seemed like a caricature of how sexy women used to be portrayed in movies that were now considered misogynistic? Why would he devote his life to an enterprise that, while arguably levelheaded, would seem to personify the most unrealistic fears of free-speech absolutists? Why didn't he like jazz anymore? Was jazz symbolic of a past he now wanted to destroy? Didn't that seem a little too nakedly symbolic? Why did he have to live in a secret apartment above a secret bar that didn't even understand its own secrecy? It wasn't like he was murdering people. Nobody goes to prison for damaging the legacy of Smashing Pumpkins. And what, exactly, was the problem with Smashing Pumpkins? How could he ethically justify committing a crime, minor or otherwise, if one of the principal results was the eradication of Billy Corgan from the historical record? It's not like anyone was forcing kids to memorize the lyrics to *Siamese Dream* in middle school. It seemed mean-spirited, and arbitrary, and also a bit loony. He steals his kid's algorithm and moves 2,800 miles away? He assumes his teenage sons will be cool with all this, simply because his girlfriend is radical and hot? The Internet works everywhere. Why not stay in Seattle and do this from an apartment in Capitol Hill? Did it never occur to Marvin that what he was doing was simultaneously self-righteous and solipsistic, and that his willingness to publicize those qualities in a local magazine pretty much proved the insincerity of his intentions?

I ask him all of those questions, almost exactly as I have outlined them here. I never even wait for the answers. Every time he tries to talk, I pose a different query. When I finally finish, he smiles. He smiles just like before, the way I'd seen him smile back in the ass doctor's waiting room. No awkwardness. No tension. I didn't know this person, but I hadn't known him for so long that it was almost like I didn't need to.

"I think you're a bit like Donna," said Marvin. "I don't think this is something you can really understand. Which isn't your fault. It's not a question of intelligence. You're a smart guy. You're smart enough to realize that this is important. You just can't fully grasp the reason why."

"That's condescending," I say.

"Maybe so," said Marvin. "But you're the kind of guy who loves mashed potatoes. Right?"

"Quit saying that. My desires don't define me. Quit bringing that up."

"But it's true."

"What does that have to do with anything?"

The door to the kitchen that looked like a bedroom swung open. Reckless Opportunist walked out into the living room, smiling and wearing only a T-shirt and panties, carrying a huge vat of garlic mashed potatoes. I wanted to cry. I wanted to punch someone. But what could I do? Some things don't change.

The Enemy Within

SHE WAS NOT UNDER ARREST. THEY TOLD HER THAT AT LEAST twenty times. She was not under arrest, she was not in danger, and they were all on her side. They only needed to ask a few questions. Her captors did not wear uniforms or masks, nor did they provide identification. They gently shoved her into the backseat of a Toyota Prius and drove to an anonymous brick building in an undisclosed location. They entered the building through a side door that led to a basement, poorly ventilated and sparsely furnished. The leader (or at least the person who appeared to be leading) told her to sit anywhere she liked, but he pointed toward one particular chair as he said this. He offered her a LaCroix, which she declined.

"Your name is Cookie Dupree," he said with the upspeak of a question.

"Yes," she replied.

"You live at 1332 Weathervane Lane," he said, again with the upspeak.

"Yes."

"You live with a man named Henry Skrabble."

"Yes," she said. "Henry is my boyfriend."

Her captors ricocheted glances. One began furiously typing into her phone. Another crossed his arms and exhaled. The leader seemed to relax.

"That's good, Cookie. Thanks for being so straightforward," he said. "I need to ask some questions about Henry Skrabble. Answer these questions honestly. It will only take a few minutes, and then you can leave. Nothing untoward will happen to you, regardless of what you say. This is a safe place. We are not the Symbionese Liberation Army. You are not Patty Hearst. No one is ending up in the closet."

Cookie wasn't sure why she believed him, but she did. Maybe it was his voice. It was the right timbre for a nonviolent hostage situation: earnest and sincere, but also respectful, but also intelligent, but also monotone, but also similar to the tenor one uses when addressing a child.

"Let's begin," said the leader. "Are you aware of the television programs Henry likes to watch on his laptop computer?"

"The television programs?"

"When he's going to sleep," said the leader. "When he's in bed, watching TV on his thirteen-inch MacBook Air, preparing to sleep. Can you identify which specific programs he prefers to watch?"

"I . . . I think I can."

"Do these TV shows, of which there are obviously many, include that series about the transgender family, or that show about young women in Brooklyn, or the show about hip-hop artists living in Georgia, or the show about the woman who kills for pleasure, or the show where the protagonist and the antagonist are the same person? These are his favorite shows, correct? When asked to list his favorite TV shows on various social media platforms, these are the shows he typically lists. Correct?"

"I'm not sure," said Cookie. "Maybe. Probably. I mean, he definitely watched shows like that, when they were on. We both did. But I don't think they're even on anymore. Are they still on?"

"That's irrelevant," said the leader. "Now, can you tell me why he liked these television programs?"

Cookie squinted.

"What was his reasoning?" asked the leader. "Did he think they were entertaining, or did he think they were necessary? Did he appreciate who was creating those shows and the perspective they offered, particularly when those perspectives contradicted his preexisting views? Did you sense his expressed affinity for these shows was, on some level, a form of signaling? When he spoke to you in private about these TV programs, what did he say?"

"I don't recall," said Cookie. "Maybe all of those things? We didn't really *talk* about those shows. We just watched them. We followed the stories."

Her captors seemed neither pleased nor alarmed by this response, although one of them sighed twice.

"Let's try again," said the leader, less reassuring than before. "What would Henry classify as more violent: physically assaulting a bad person, or anecdotally invalidating a good person?"

"Maybe equal," she said. "Henry is not a violent man. He abhors violence. In fact, whenever violence is discussed, he specifically uses the word *abhor*. He stopped watching football on principle."

"Aha," said the leader. "But tell me this: Did you *notice* that he stopped watching football, or did you overhear him *telling other people* that he stopped watching football? Did it seem like he *wanted* people to know he doesn't watch football? Did he claim it was because of the concussions, or did he claim it was because of what football represents? Did it have anything to do with players' kneeling during the national anthem?"

"I don't know," said Cookie. "We don't even have a real TV."

One of the captors threw a phone across the room. The leader glared at her and she nonverbally apologized.

"Sorry about that," said the leader. "That was unacceptable. Like I said, this is a safe place. It's not a place where we throw technology. But—having said that—you do need to try a little harder, Cookie. You need to compromise. These are not invasive queries. Your answers don't need to be complete or absolute or provable. They just need to help us understand what we are trying to understand. Do you understand that?"

"I'm trying," said Cookie.

"I know you are. And that's all that matters. Trying is all that matters," said the leader. "Tell me this: Has he ever explained something to you that you already knew?"

"Like about what?"

"Like about anything."

"Well, of course. We've been together seven years. He's constantly telling me how to sort the recycling. Which, I'll admit, is pretty complicated in our building. More complicated than it should be. But not so complicated that I need to be told every other month. You know what I mean? The bins are labeled. The compost goes in the blue bin. Or maybe the green bin? Either way, I can figure it out."

"Absolutely," said the leader. "I know how that feels. We totally, completely understand how that feels. How about books? Does he ever tell you to read certain books that wouldn't normally interest you?"

"Actually, yes. He has done that quite often," said Cookie. "And it's annoying, although sometimes his suggestions are okay. That Norwegian guy was good, for a while. But can you please just tell me why you need to know this? Was Henry in an accident?"

"It's a bit more serious than that," said the leader. "We have reason to believe your boyfriend is Fake Woke."

For an endless second, loud silence.

"That's impossible," Cookie finally spat. "Henry? There is no way Henry is the person you think he is. You should see his browser history.

You should hear the way he talks about Rachel Dolezal. We wouldn't be together if what you're saying were true. I'm not some Eva Braun."

The band of captors took a few awkward steps toward her, surrounding Cookie on all sides. One put his hand on her shoulder, only to remove it when another captor noticed how inappropriate it was to do so.

"I realize this is a hard tablet to swallow," said the leader. "It's a terrible thing to reconcile. And I know you see how Henry acts at home, and how he behaves at the food co-op, and I'm sure you follow his Twitter feed. And you know, maybe he is the person you think he is. Maybe we're overreacting. But I don't think so. Evidence to the contrary is mounting. You're not the first person we've spoken with. You might be stunned by some of the things Henry has said to his friends and to his therapist and to his barber."

Cookie's cosmos began to collapse. She loved Henry, but he did seem to get way too many haircuts. Should she defend him to these strangers, or would that make her part of the problem? Should she claim she didn't care about the accusations, or was apathy a form of compliance?

"Let me talk to him," said Cookie. "He will respond to reason. He deserves that chance. I mean, I don't know. Maybe he is what you say. Maybe he is. I don't know. Anything is possible. But at least he's *presenting* the persona of someone who feels guilty about his privilege. He *acts* like he's guilty. That must count for something, right? Isn't pretending better than nothing at all?"

"No," said the leader. "It's a thousand times worse."

Cookie dropped her head and began to weep. She knew he was right.

The Secret

THE THING YOU MUST ACCEPT," MARSH EXPLAINED FOR THE THIRD time, "is that this is not a job you can quit. You need to understand that. You can be fired, but you can't quit."

"I understand," said Cope. "I would never quit. I've never quit anything in my life."

"That response proves you still don't understand," said Marsh. "That response tells me you aren't really listening. The issue is not your depth of commitment. The issue is that you can't quit, under any circumstances, even if quitting seems like the only moral or logical move. That option does not exist. You can request that we terminate you, and—sometimes—that request is granted. But quitting is not your decision. When and if you retire is not your decision."

Cope wanted to ask how such a fascist policy could possibly be enforced. But he also knew asking such a question was not what he was supposed to do, and that whatever ambiguous answer Marsh provided would only generate more questions, and that on some guttural level he already knew the truth, anyway.

"You're not a normal person," Marsh continued. "I suppose it could be argued that there are no quote-unquote *normal* people, and that *normal* is a meaningless modifier. But that's an argument for college kids. You know what I mean. You would not be here if you were just another goofball. We would not have reached this point in the process. That said—you have, for the most part, lived a normal life. You do a lot of normal things in a normal way. That ends today. And don't tell me you're excited about that, because you can't possibly comprehend what it means. I know you think you don't want to be normal. I didn't want to be normal. Nobody does. But not being normal is not what you imagine. A movie star is still a normal person. The president is still a normal person. They are allowed the luxury of thoughtlessness."

This, thought Cope, was bordering on overkill. Was Marsh trying to impress him? Was he trying to scare him? It was actually a bit insulting. He didn't know exactly what he was getting into, but he knew enough to understand the limitations of federal employment. Would he learn some troubling things? Probably. Would he learn some things the president didn't know? Hopefully. It's not like the president knows everything. Nobody knows everything.

"So this is your last chance," said Marsh. "And I say that knowing you would never say no to this opportunity. I can tell just by looking at you. But I still have to ask the question and I still have to make the offer. If you want to decline, this is the time to decline."

"I want this," said Cope. "Whatever it is."

"Then follow me."

They walked down the hall to the elevator bank. They stepped into the same elevator Cope had taken every morning for the past two years and descended past the lobby, into the basement. Cope had been in the basement before; there was nothing secret about the basement. But there was an innocuous black door near the furnace room that Cope had never previously noticed, and Marsh used a digital key to open it up. They stepped through the black door and into a poorly lit hallway. The hallway led to another bank of elevators, maybe twenty steps away. They boarded an elevator and descended again, this time at a much higher rate of speed. When it finally stopped and the doors slid open, they stepped out into an antiseptic foyer that was bright and empty, except for one thing—another single elevator, this one circular, built into the middle of the floor. They entered the third elevator and plunged again, slowly. The ride lasted almost two minutes.

"How deep are we underground?" asked Cope.

"Forty-five feet," said Marsh.

"Forty-five floors?"

"Forty-five feet."

"That can't be right," said Cope. But Marsh didn't even look at him.

The elevator door twisted open and they stepped out into a room so large that Cope wasn't sure it could even be classified as a room. The mammoth space was divided into hundreds of smaller chambers, but all the dividing walls were plexiglass. Nothing was hidden or obscured (including the room containing the toilets and the tampon dispensers). Most of the cubicles contained robotic contraptions and oversized computers, along with perhaps a hundred human employees in lab coats shuffling from location to location. The most perplexing room was the first one Cope noticed. It was occupied by twenty-four haggard humans, all of whom were flipping coins and manually recording the results of each toss into the pages of a binder. Cope could not even manage a cogent question. He just pointed at the people and stared at Marsh with a combination of disgust and astonishment.

"I'll just jump right into this. That's usually the best way," said Marsh. "Over the next three hundred or so seconds, I'm going to tell you several things that will make you crazy. You will want to interrupt me and ask questions, and your questions will be reasonable. Resist that urge. In all probability, the questions you want to ask are the same questions we're trying to answer."

Cope listened. He said nothing. He did not, however, stop pointing at the two dozen people flipping coins.

"That's Group B," said Marsh, nodding toward the humans. "Group A is the room over there, perpendicular to Group B. Group C is the room to our immediate left. As you can see, Group A is a collection of twenty-four robotic arms that flip coins perpetually, one flip every eight seconds. That's ten thousand eight hundred mechanical coin flips per machine, every day, multiplied by twenty-four units. Group C is just a Cray supercomputer, an older one from the nineties. All it does is *simulate* the flipping of a coin, roughly two hundred ninety thousand times a second, nonstop, three hundred sixty-five days a year. Group B, as you've obviously noticed, is comprised of twenty-four living-and-breathing people, flipping actual coins in the conventional way people have always flipped coins. They work at their own pace, eight hours a day, five days a week. A solid performance for a dedicated employee is roughly two thousand flips per shift."

"Who are they?" asked Cope.

"That's not my department," he said. "All I know is that these are folks from all walks of life who have committed crimes that are not technically illegal, but who nonetheless realize that public knowledge of these non-illegal crimes would almost certainly get them killed, or worse. So this is the compromise we make. They sign NDAs and do this instead. We protect them, and we pay way more than minimum wage. It's recession-proof. We provide them with decent downtown apartments. I'm sure it's boring work, but lots of jobs are boring. And at least they're doing something important, even if they don't know why."

"How is this possibly important?"

"Let me ask you something," said Marsh. "I mentioned how the Cray supercomputer simulates two hundred ninety thousand coin flips every second. That being the case, how many of those flips should result in an outcome of Heads and how many should result in an outcome of Tails?"

"Is this question rhetorical?" asked Cope.

"It's not rhetorical," said Marsh, "and your unspoken answer is, of course, correct, plus-or-minus a few thousand flips that will drift toward equilibrium over time. This is the bedrock principle of probability: Coins have no memory, the next flip is always fifty-fifty, and all that contingency shit. The world is built on this. So let me ask you a similar question about the robots with robot arms in Group A and the humans with human arms in Group B. If a robot flips a coin two hundred ninety thousand times, or if a person flips a coin two hundred ninety thousand times, how many of those flips will result in an outcome of Heads and how many will result in an outcome of Tails?"

"Can't you just tell me what's really happening here?" asked Cope. "You obviously know I'm going to say one hundred forty-five thousand, and I already know my answer must be wrong, because you wouldn't be asking the question if the rational answer was the actual answer."

"What's really happening here," said Marsh, "is that the universe is unraveling. That's what's happening here. Now are you going to shut up and listen? You have no idea how stupid you are right now. At this moment, your mind is very small. It's a mouse mind. When we got into that elevator, you were smart. But now you're an idiot. You are currently the dumbest person you know. There is no thought you've ever had that I didn't have five years before it occurred to you."

Cope's natural inclination was to respond with sarcasm. He knew he was smart. That was the only thing he knew for sure. *The Fresno Bee* had once referred to him as a "wunderkind." But then again, he was currently watching twenty-four people flipping coins in a secret underground bunker, and this (apparently) was critical to his new life. He was, at the very minimum, smart enough to know that this was not a time for sarcasm. He affected obedience to the best of his abilities.

"A simulated coin toss is a fifty-fifty proposition," continued Marsh. "A real coin toss is not. Not anymore. It used to be, but now it's not. And no one knows why. And no, it's not the weight distribution of the coin. We factored that in and fixed it. And it has nothing to do with which side of the coin happens to face upward at the inception of the toss. We factored that in, too. Fifteen years ago, we realized analog coin flips were coming up Tails at a rate just over fifty-one percent. We couldn't deny the statistics no matter how hard we tried. Today it's almost fifty-five percent, and not just here in the lab. Everywhere. We started tracking the coin toss from every pro and college football game in North America and pretty much every soccer match in Europe. The percentages continue to line up. Nobody notices, because nobody flips a coin enough times to see trends. Nobody else cares, thank God."

Marsh hugged himself, still looking at the human flippers. Cope tried not to smirk.

"And now," continued Marsh, "unless I've totally misread you, we've reached the point in the conversation where you will start asking your dumb-fuck dismissive questions. So go ahead and do that. Let's get it out of the way. Ask me something foolish."

"My pleasure," said Cope. "This is the scary monster the president can't know about? This is the covert history of existence? Are you kidding me? I can't imagine what it must have cost to build this place, or to keep it functioning. This has to be the most fiscally irresponsible experiment since Apollo, not to mention a pretty egregious manifestation of low-level white slavery. *'The universe is unraveling.'* Is that how everybody talks down here? I'm pretty sure the universe will not unravel if somebody flips a coin twenty times and only gets nine Heads. I'm pretty sure the universe will not give a shit. But I can tell from your facial expression that you knew this is what I was going to say, so please tell me why I'm a moron."

Marsh kept staring into the plexiglass, unwilling to look Cope in the face. Marsh knew this was how the tutorial would go. It always went like this. Maybe it had to. Maybe it was the only way.

"Do you believe the things I'm telling you?" asked Marsh.

"I don't know," said Cope. "About the coins? I don't know. I suppose I believe you. Am I not supposed to believe you? Is that the test?"

"What you believe, in other words, is that something that should be a fifty-fifty proposition is not a fifty-fifty proposition. What you believe, in other words, is that something that has always been true just stopped being true, without justification."

"Yes," said Cope. "I do. Isn't that why I'm here? Because of my work on Mpemba?" Years ago, as a Stanford grad student, Cope had achieved a modicum of academic fame for his dissertation on the Mpemba effect, a phenomenon that occasionally (and inexplicably) causes hot water to freeze at a faster rate than cold water. "That's what I do, and that's why I'm here: to justify what can't be justified, just like I did with Mpemba."

"You're not getting it," said Marsh. "This is not that. We are not missing some overlooked, undiscovered detail. There are no details down here. It's people flipping coins. It's robots flipping coins. It's a computer pretending to flip coins. It's something that can only work one way, which is the only way it's ever worked. And then, at some point, it stopped working. And we have to figure out why that happened. And it can't just be an interesting theory. We have to know, for real."

"I'm not sure that we do," said Cope. "I mean, this is interesting. I'm definitely interested. But I don't see how understanding the discrepancy is essential. It's a math issue. It has to be a mathematical anomaly. Since when does the government care about math?"

"It's not math," said Marsh. "Or at least it's not *only* math. It's something else. The coin flips aren't the point. The coin flips are just the emergent manifestation of the perception shift."

"Okay. Wonderful. What does that mean?"

"It means exactly what the words imply. And it means you can't talk about what's going on down here, to anyone. Ever."

"Talk about what? That there are secret people working underground, flipping coins for no reason?"

"How deep are we underground, Cope?"

Cope suddenly knew the answer to that question, and not just because Marsh had told him a few minutes prior. He somehow knew the answer on his own terms, and the answer made sense to him, even if every other experience he'd ever had told him otherwise. He thought about this for a long time, or for what seemed like a long time. It was becoming difficult to tell how long a minute was supposed to be.

"Wait," said Cope. "This doesn't track. I didn't know any of this when I got off the elevator, so how could it be that—"

"Because I knew," said Marsh. "You didn't need to know, because I knew. Which is why your life is fucked now, just like my life is fucked. I'm sorry. I'm sorry you agreed to do this. You should have said no. You will regret not saying no. But that regret is something you need to get over, right now. Today. There is no going back, and we need you for this. If we figure this out, maybe everything returns to the way it was. Maybe it stops. Maybe we stop it. But until that happens, the only means of containment is absolute silence. It doesn't happen to people who don't know it's happening."

"What doesn't happen?"

"Have you read *The Secret*? It's like that."

"Have I read the what? It's like the what?"

"Thoughts become things," said Marsh. "That part of the book is actually true."

"This is nonsense," said Cope, trying to supplant his fear with testosterone. "This is not what I thought it was going to be."

"You're right. It's not."

"I don't want to be involved with this."

"I don't either. But that option is no longer available."

"I want to get out of here."

"That's understandable," said Marsh. "You will need some time with this. Go home. Have a drink. But don't get drunk. For the rest of your life, never get drunk."

"Do I take the same elevators back up?"

"You don't need the elevators," said Marsh. "Take the stairs." He pointed toward another black door, identical to the one from the basement. "I will see you here tomorrow. Show up early, or show up at noon. It works either way."

Cope walked to the door as fast as he could, but not so fast as to seem like a person on the verge of panic. He opened the black door and started up the concrete stairwell. It was four short flights. It was a thirty-second climb. When he reached the top and pushed open the exit, he found himself in the parking garage, across the street from his old office building. It took him twenty-nine minutes to find his car. He drove home on streets he barely recognized. They were the same streets with the same names, but the topography was different. All the road signs were in kilometers. He tried to find something familiar on the radio, but even the classic rock station was playing songs he could not recall. He reached his suburban duplex and parked in the driveway. He sat in the car longer than necessary and wondered if he was about to vomit. Did his house look the same as it had that morning? He thought that it did, but he wasn't certain. It was an odd sensation, this uncertainty about his own house. He eventually got out from behind the wheel and walked to the front door. He worried that his key would not work, but it did, although the door opened into the kitchen instead of the living room. He saw an Asian woman washing dishes. It was a woman he'd dated in college, twice.

"Hey, bae," said the woman. She didn't look up from the suds.

"Hi," said Cope. "Hello."

"What happened to the garbage disposal? Did you break it again?"

"I have no idea," said Cope. "Probably. Yes."

Trial and Error

SHE BELIEVED SHE COULD SOLVE HER PROBLEMS BY KILLING A wolf. That's how it was in those days. It was something that was questioned and debated, but generally internalized and accepted. Not everyone believed killing a wolf was a viable solution to any problem that had no answer, but enough people did to make it reasonable. You would never be viewed as eccentric for killing a wolf. In fact, some might make the accusation if you didn't at least consider the possibility.

She used to believe she could solve her problems on her own, back when she was younger and less terrified of her limitations. Her friends insisted this was all within her control—isolate each issue, drill down to the core, fix what is fixable, endure what is not. But her problems were not like that. She was lonely. She longed to be in a relationship, specifically with the one person who appeared to understand the dark feelings she never dared to express. This person, however, was already married and used his understanding to manipulate her. Her best qualities made her vulnerable. She was able to make a little money doing what she enjoyed, but it wasn't enough money. She needed to make a lot more money in order to pay for the things she'd purchased when she was broke, so she took a job that was boring and sometimes humiliating. There was no way around this. There was no other job to take. She constantly felt ill, but doctors were mystified as to why (and sometimes seemed to accuse her of lying, although never directly). Her parents longed to help but only made things worse, suffocating her with unwanted attention that sowed envy and resentment among her siblings. There was simply no escape from the life she had assembled by accident. There were no analytical conversations or tiers of self-reflection that would resolve her dilemmas. It was time to try something radical. It was time to kill the wolf.

She knew of several people who had killed wolves in order to improve their lives, but only one of these people was a close enough friend to ask for advice. They met in a tavern. He explained how his business had failed and how his wife had deserted him, so he killed a wolf. Now he had a new job and a new wife. His new wife had also killed a wolf, just before they began dating.

She asked how the wolf had been killed. He said he had used the traditional method: He covered a sharpened knife in pig's blood, placed the knife in his freezer, and allowed the blood to freeze into ice. The frozen blade was then doused with another coating of pig's blood and frozen again. He repeated this process forty times, until the knife had become a crimson pork popsicle. A final coat of fresh blood was applied to the surface of the ice, just before he positioned the blade upright on the forest floor. A wolf, smelling the fresh blood, discovered the camouflaged knife and commenced licking its savory frozen coating. Over time, the wolf stripped away the ice and exposed the blade, but the ice had numbed the animal's tongue. The wolf did not realize the knife was now slicing into his anesthetized mouth; instead, the wolf tasted his own warm blood and licked even harder. This continued until the wolf, weakened by his actions and conditioned by his desire, slowly bled out.

She found this description disturbing. She also found it preposterous. It did not seem like a practical way to kill anything, unless wolves were far dumber than she'd always believed. She was embarrassed by the depth of her desperation. How could a dead wolf solve any problem that wasn't wolf-related? If it worked, it worked. She'd do it if it worked, no matter how brutal or implausible. But how would it work? Why would it work? "I don't know if it necessarily does," her friend said, immune to the consequence of his confession. "I can't prove any undeniable relationship between what I did and what happened in my life. It's possible I murdered a wolf for no reason. But I'd do it again, and so would my wife. If we end up having kids and my kids have problems, I will absolutely advise them to kill a wolf. I will give them my knife and pay for the pig blood."

She did not find his reasoning persuasive. She would not kill a wolf. She was not going to pretend to believe something insane, based on the minuscule possibility that accepting such insanity might work to her advantage.

She told him she had changed her mind. "That's fine," he replied. "But you're looking at this with the wrong kind of certitude. I don't know if I believe that killing a wolf does anything, or that whatever it supposedly achieves is somehow related to making life better than it already is. It probably makes some lives worse. Maybe it made my life worse. Maybe I shouldn't have a job at all. Maybe I'm not that good at the thing I think I'm good at. Maybe I shouldn't be married to anyone. Maybe my first wife left me because I'm the kind of guy who doesn't need a valid reason to kill a wolf. But I need to do something, and I have to live somewhere, and I don't want to live by myself, and I don't want to die alone. I want a certain type of life, and it seems like the wolf killers get that life. So I killed the wolf. I froze the blood and planted the knife. I did the weird thing that was required. I don't know how much it matters if I don't believe in the weird thing. It's something that people do, and I'm a person, and I prefer to be with the other people."

She listened to his story and nodded politely. She thanked him for his time and walked home. She returned to her apartment and went to bed, fantasizing about the married man she hated to love and dreading the mind-numbing work that would await her tomorrow morning. Her creditors would be in contact. Her parents would want to know how she was feeling and why she wasn't getting better. Tomorrow would be another horrible day, as would the day after that and the day after that.

She would kill a wolf, someday. She'd already mentally selected the knife she'd freeze. She understood who she was, below the surface. But she wouldn't kill the wolf tomorrow, or the day after that, or the day after that. It would take a long time, and it would take even longer before she'd quit wondering why she was no longer miserable.

Tricks Aren't Illusions

IT WAS SNOWING WHEN HE AWOKE AND IT WAS STILL SNOWING NOW. It was snowing so hard that every window became more interesting than the television. Like every other nonessential employee, he had been warned to stay away from the office. They told him to work from home, so he checked Slack on his phone while flipping through a coffee table book about prehistoric mammals. It was a long eight hours, but not long enough. Now he was boiling tricolor rotini and warming a jar of organic pomodoro sauce on the stove, staring down at the empty white streets from his kitchen window and fantasizing about staying home again tomorrow, or at least staying home until noon. The fantasy was interrupted by three knocks at the door, fast and loud. He assumed it was his elderly neighbor from down the hall, because no one had buzzed the downstairs buzzer. But when he opened the door, it was Keith, looking like a man who'd died descending Everest.

"How did you get in?"

"The downstairs door is ajar," said Keith. "There's a snowdrift in your lobby."

"How'd you get here? Are the subways running?"

"I drove," said Keith.

"Why the fuck did you drive?"

"I have a problem," said Keith.

Keith removed his black peacoat and shook off the snow in the hall-way. He took off his black seventy-five-cent thrift-store stocking cap and his black cowhide work gloves and his black Rag & Bone boots and his red cashmere scarf. There was a duffel bag at his side, which he tossed onto a chair as he stepped through the doorway. He used the bathroom without closing the door and asked over his shoulder if there was anything to eat. They sat in the living room with matching bowls of pasta. Keith shoveled forkfuls into his mouth with the shameless focus of a teenager. He declined a beer. He declined an offer to get high. He said he didn't want to play Xbox or listen to the Doors or watch the Weather Channel. These were troubling signs.

"Why are you here?"

"Why am I here?"

"Yeah. What's happening?"

"I need your help," said Keith. "The BQE is closed. The West Side Highway is closed above Fourteenth and the tunnel is closed completely. I need to stay here tonight. I'll leave as soon as anything opens."

"Where are you going?"

"Before I explain," said Keith, "I need you to think about everything you know about me."

"I need to do what?"

"Just think about everything you know about me," said Keith. "Who am I? What am I like?"

"You're the kind of person who shows up unannounced during a snowstorm and won't explain why."

"Indulge me," said Keith.

"That's what I'm doing."

"No, you're not. Not really," said Keith. "I need you to think about who I am. You know me. Think about the person you know."

He did know Keith. That was undeniable. He'd known him for fourteen years, after college but before either had moved to the city, back when they were both trying to become professional magicians. It seemed so ridiculous, in retrospect, that this had been their shared aspiration. But that was who they used to be. They would constantly run into each other at clubs on the outskirts of Las Vegas, almost always working for free, almost always finishing their sets around the time it made sense to drink coffee and eat pancakes. They were terrible magicians. They didn't realize how terrible until they became roommates and had to reconcile the fact that working the same places at the same times meant they were the same level of dismal. They lived together for eighteen months before Keith decided failing in California was better than failing in Nevada. He moved to L.A. in the middle of the night on Halloween. They spoke on the phone the following week, then again the following month, and then lost contact for the next three years. There was no dispute. There were no hard feelings. It was pure male laziness. He did not expect to see Keith again, which bothered him (although not enough to stop it from happening). He gave up on magic when his parents died in a fire. He took the insurance money and moved to Manhattan, a move intended to eliminate the possibility of running into anyone he knew. He didn't want to explain who he was or what had happened. But Keith was already there, somehow, managing a used book store in the same gentrified neighborhood as his sublet. They'd both become different people, and a different kind of friendship instantly resumed. It wasn't like Vegas at all.

They were no longer irresponsible or ambitious, they never complained about the price of doves or rabbits, and there were no drunken arguments about the ethics of Val Valentino. Magic was never referenced, even in jest. It was like that part of their lives had never happened, despite being the genesis for everything between them.

They did New Yorkish things together, particularly things that were social and sedentary and vaguely cosmopolitan. It was a high-volume, low-impact relationship. Keith was an easy person to know, mostly because Keith was unusually willing to discuss all the contradictory qualities he believed made him unknowable. He always gave spare change to the homeless while habitually classifying those who contributed to institutional charities as misguided sheeple. He believed the clearest gauge of any musical group's significance was the moral clarity of its fan base, so he forced himself to love the Mekons and Pussy Riot. He was against abortion, the death penalty, and the space program. Virtually all of his short-lived girlfriends were black, but he didn't have a single black male friend. He was a hospice volunteer. He hated dogs. He was obsessed with politics but never voted. He didn't care about money, but he also didn't make much money, so it was difficult to understand how he always had plenty of money on the rare occasions he wanted to spend a lot of it. Once, seated at a restaurant with five other people, he declared that he would happily donate a kidney to anyone he knew, with no qualms and no questions asked. But his expressed motive for doing so was problematic, in that this pledge hinged on the condition that everyone he knew would be obligated to remember he had done this and thereby view the rest of his personality through the prism of this one specific generosity. He was a glutton, but the kind of glutton who offered to wash the dishes.

"Okay. I'm doing it. I'm thinking about who you are."

"Good," said Keith. "Now tell me this: Do you consider me to be a reasonable person?"

"Not especially."

"But do I at least *employ* reason when I make decisions? Even if you disagree with my reasoning, do you concede that some level of reasoning was involved?"

"I suppose."

"And would you concede," Keith continued, "that I'm a *good* person? Do you consider me a moral person?"

"Well, you're technically my best friend, so . . ."

"So?"

"So I wouldn't classify my best friend as a bad person. I wouldn't have a best friend who was a bad person. That would be hard to justify."

Keith stood up and padded into the kitchen. It felt like he was in there for a long time, in light of the circumstances and the imprecise gravity of the conversation. When he returned to the living room, he had another bowl of pasta, along with an unwrapped piece of coffee cake.

"Here's the two-pronged situation," said Keith. "I can't tell you what my problem is, and I'm going to eat this coffee cake, if that's cool with you. It's from Starbucks, right?"

"It is. But you have to tell me what the problem is. Otherwise you can't have the cake."

"I can't tell you my problem," said Keith. "For your own protection. It's better if you don't know. I don't want to implicate you, and I don't want to put you in a position where you need to lie to someone else."

"Did you kill somebody?"

"Let's say that I did," said Keith. "Would you want to know that?"

"You killed someone."

"I didn't say I killed someone," said Keith. "I said *let's say* I killed someone. Let's just pretend that I did. If that happened, if I killed some-one, why would you assume I did that? What would be my motive?"

"I have no idea. But I also can't tell what we're actually talking about, so . . ."

"You've known me a long time," said Keith. "We're friends. Best friends, as you yourself have specified. And as you noted, you wouldn't have a best friend who was a bad person. So let me ask you this: In all the years we've known each other, have I done anything that would lead you to believe that I would kill another person?"

"On purpose? Not on purpose."

"But I'm a reasonable man," said Keith. "That's been established. You said so yourself. If a reasonable man killed someone accidentally, he would not flee the city in the dead of night. T or F? A reasonable man would call the police and explain what happened."

"What I actually said was that you were not especially reasonable."

"But you were joking, because you didn't really know what we were talking about," said Keith. "And you did grant that I *employ* reason. You believe I'm a good person who employs reason, the kind of person who has never exhibited any desire or aptitude to kill. So if that *did* happen—if I *did* kill someone—it would have to be a reasonable, justifiable act. Any other scenario would contradict every other thing you know about me. You said so yourself. You openly said you would not be best friends with an unreasonable murderer."

"Unless I didn't know that the friend in question was both unreason-able and murderous."

"But how could that be?" asked Keith. "How could you not recognize something that profound? What is more likely: that the past fourteen years have been false, or that this current moment—though atypical—still jibes with your lived experience?"

"The answer to that question is irrelevant. I'm not going to sit here and conclude that it's okay if you hypothetically killed someone, simply because we've been friends for fourteen years and you haven't killed anyone before."

"Here again, I did not say I killed someone," said Keith. "But that's a rough equivalency."

"Did you rape someone?"

"Jesus, of course not. I can't believe you'd even say that."

"Well, I don't know of a lot of other crimes that are roughly equivalent to murder. If you won't tell me what happened, what am I supposed to think? You still work in a fucking bookstore. You're not exactly well positioned to commit treason."

"This is precisely why I can't tell you my problem," said Keith. "If you have no idea what happened, if you can't even guess—that's to your advantage. You have plausible deniability, in the truest sense of the definition: A reasonable, moral friend barged into your home during a nor'easter. You offered him pasta. He ate a piece of store-purchased coffee cake. He slept on your couch. You thought it was strange. His behavior annoyed you, because you were saving the coffee cake for tomorrow. But that's all you know, and you can express that lack of knowledge with honesty. From your perspective, there's nothing else to the story. It's not airtight logic, but it's a form of logic. Agree or disagree? T or F?"

It was almost nine o'clock. He could not kick Keith out into the weather, nor could he prove that Keith had done anything warranting expulsion. He would never call the police, he wouldn't have anything to tell them if he did, and they wouldn't show up during a blizzard, anyway. Moreover, bad-faith reasoning appealed to his sympathies. He saw himself as the kind of guy who would always help a friend who needed help, even if that friend didn't necessarily deserve it. In fact, especially if that friend didn't deserve it. A friend who didn't deserve help was indeed a friend in need. It's easy to do the right thing when you believe what you are doing is right. It's harder when you have no idea. They were still arguing, but it wasn't a real argument. Keith was staying. There had never been any doubt in either of their minds.

"I won't ask where you're going, since I know you won't tell me. But what will you do? How will you live?"

Keith pointed toward his duffel bag on the chair. It was massive. It was designed for hockey players.

"That's filled with money?"

"No," said Keith. "Equipment. Some of which is still probably yours."

"You're kidding."

"It's a viable vocation," said Keith.

"Not if you're bad at it. Not if you haven't done it for ten years."

"Maybe I got better," said Keith. "Maybe that's what this is really about. Maybe that's why I'm here. I would never say that, of course, even if it were true. Especially if it were true, considering the circumstances."

"Maybe that's why you're here."

"Yes," said Keith. "Maybe."

"You maybe murdered a guy with magic."

"I did not say that. But if I did, would it even count as murder?"

"Yes. It would."

"I'm not so sure," said Keith. "It would depend on the circumstance."

"Such as?"

"A person sees a trick that is so shocking they have a heart attack. A person assisting with a dangerous illusion panics and makes a critical error. A person is duped by a magician and responds in anger, so the magician is forced to violently defend himself. An attempt at levitation goes awry and someone falls out of an open window. A person gets involved with real magic and is killed telepathically. A magician takes over another person's body through astral projection."

"Those are all examples of murder, or at least manslaughter. Those are also examples of tricks you could never possibly perform, or even attempt, because you're terrible at magic. Also, two of those examples are theoretically impossible, which doesn't bolster your argument."

"Everyone is bad at everything," said Keith, "until they get better. And everything is impossible until somebody does it once."

"You did not kill anyone with magic."

"I never said that I did."

This went on for another two hours. It was just like Vegas. They even took some shots at Val Valentino. You miss old friends when you don't see them, but you miss them more when you do. There are good people and there are bad people, and that should make a difference. Good people do good things. Bad people do bad things. That should dictate who we care about. And it does, but only when being a person matters more than being a friend.

"I'm going to bed."

"I think the snow is dissipating," said Keith. "I might be able to leave before sunrise."

"Are you going to kill me while I sleep?"

"Of course not," said Keith. "Murder does not come naturally to me."

"Will I ever see you again?"

"I certainly hope so," said Keith as he reclined on the couch. "But no."

He used the bathroom, washed his face, and retired to the bedroom. He lay in the dark for a long time, wondering what Keith had done, wondering if he was now doing something equally bad, wondering what it meant to be a person who truly did not judge, lest he be judged. When he awoke, the sun was pouring through his window, the plows had plowed, the cars were crawling along the freeways, and the magician had vanished.

Fluke

TO SAY HE WASN'T HAVING FUN WOULD BE IMPRECISE. IT WAS pleasant, what they were doing: drinking cold wine, making mean jokes about popular podcasts, listening to songs from artists that had once seemed essential but now seemed absurd. If he could spend a vacation doing anything, these are the activities he would choose. But tonight he was only pretending to be happy, and he feared the others could tell he wasn't listening to the conversation, even when he himself was talking. There were other things on his mind. He didn't need friends right now. He got up from the rocking chair and disappeared through the screen door that led to the beach. He could hear his wife asking why he was going out into the rain, but he didn't look back and behaved as if he'd heard nothing at all.

The drizzle was negligible, almost a mist. It would be an hour before it rained angry. He walked without shoes on the impossibly long wooden dock, over the dunes and out toward the water. At first, he could still hear the music from the living room mixed with the voices of the various couples, particularly the donkey laugh of his old pal Roger. By the time he reached the middle of the dock, Roger's laugh was the only sound he could decipher. When he reached the dock's end, he could hear nothing except the ocean. He was finally alone.

"You should be happy to have this problem," he kept telling himself, as if it were possible to change your feelings by criticizing your conscience. He'd received the offer Friday afternoon, just as he and Ruth were catching the ferry to Atlantique. He sheepishly passed the phone to his wife so that she could read the email. "That's amazing," she said without inflection. "What are you going to do?" He stared straight through her face, like a cow. "Let me rephrase the question," his wife said again. "What are you going to do, besides not talk about it?"

He spent the next thirty hours incessantly balancing two thoughts at the same time. The first thought would change. The second thought did not. When he was scrubbing the grill, he thought about the cleanliness of the grill, but also about his problem. When he threw a Frisbee on the beach, he thought about the velocity of the wind and the accuracy of his toss, but also about his problem. In the shower, he thought about his problem while searching for the shampoo. He never relaxed. It never went away. He took an afternoon nap and woke up exhausted. The complexities of the conundrum were so straightforward. There was no way to simplify the decision. If he accepted the offer, he would make more money. But it wouldn't be life-changing money, because that had already happened in his twenties and money can only change your life once. If he accepted the offer, he would travel constantly, often to exotic places. But traveling is only exciting if you're single. What's the upside of meeting interesting people if you're already married? His preference was to exclusively encounter people who were boring, and those people could be found in New York. If he accepted the offer, the work would be challenging and (potentially) satisfying. It would move him into a rarefied tier of his already rarefied profession. But wasn't his current mediocrity challenging enough? Wasn't his life already (potentially) satisfying? He was about to turn thirty-three. The number of years he still had to work was roughly equivalent to the number of years he'd been alive on earth. That felt like a prison sentence. Maybe if he took the offer, he could bank the money and retire at forty-five. But that would never happen. The kind of guy who took this type of offer always worked until he died, and he would become one of those guys. He probably was one of those guys already, which is why the offer was made. Besides, what good would it do to retire? He couldn't even enjoy a perfect vacation. One fortuitous problem was all it took to ruin everything.

He stared at the black ocean and felt like a child who was trying to comprehend his parents' impending divorce. What was he hoping to realize? Why was he looking at something he could barely see? All that was visible was the horizon. The waves were so dark. They were not even shapes. He could hear them more than he could see them. Every so often, a crooked bolt of lightning would slash across the sky and everything would be illuminated for half a second. For an instant, he'd see the entire beach, no differently than if it were noon. But then the bolt would vanish and the landscape would cut back to blackness, and all that remained discernible was the distant barrier between the water and the sky. He decided to go back to the house, embarrassed by his abrupt departure. It was getting colder and there was nothing to see. He started fabricating an excuse to explain why he had walked out of the house and into the darkness. But then it happened. The horizon exploded. The stasis was shattered by something huge and fast and far away. A whale. The silhouette of a humpback whale, breaching the surface before falling back into the sea. He'd never before seen a whale that wasn't on PBS. He'd never considered the possibility of seeing a whale in these waters, or even the prospect of an invisible whale lurking beneath the surface. Yet there it was. He'd been staring into nothingness for no applicable reason, and then he'd seen the unmistakable profile of a thirty-three-ton mammal pitching itself out of the ocean and into the air. This had really happened, and it had happened to him. And then, twenty seconds later, it happened again. The same whale jumped forty feet above the surface, arching its spine and twisting its torso.

Except this time, the whale was struck by lightning.

The bolt struck the beast at the apex of its breach. It appeared to freeze in space, suspended in midair like an aquatic Wile E. Coyote before dropping like an anvil. It fell into the abyss the way ducks fall from the sky when blasted with a shotgun. There was no sound to accompany the electrocution. It was too far away. All he heard was the waves hitting the shore in front of him. But he knew what he saw. This had really happened, and it had happened to him.

He scanned the horizon for another two minutes, wondering if he would somehow see the whale alive. A creature that size might be able to absorb a heavy electrical jolt. Then again, whales live in the water, which is not the ideal venue for surviving thirty thousand amps of energy. Was it dead? It was probably dead. It had to be dead. It was dead.

The drizzle started to pick up, as did the wind. He turned and walked back to the house like a blind man late for work, guiding himself along the dock's rail. The darkness had gotten thicker, bordering on scary. He only knew he was close when he heard Roger's donkey laugh. He had to get back to Roger. The screen door he'd used to exit was now latched and locked, so he jogged around to the front of the house and barged though the main entrance.

"Ruth," he said as he pushed open the door. He must have yelled her name with an alarming tone, because his wife jumped up from the couch and ran into the kitchen. "Morris? Are you okay?" she asked. "Is somebody out there?"

"Let's go up to the bedroom," he said. "We need to talk."

Back in the living room, the other three couples fell silent. They turned off the music, then quickly turned it back on in order to seem casual. Morris and Ruth moved to the upstairs room they always shared and closed the door. He sat on the bed. She elected to stand. They both looked worried for reasons neither could explain.

"What's happening?" she asked. "They're all going to think we're fighting. Are we fighting?"

"They can think what they want," said Morris. "I wanted to tell you that I'm declining the offer."

"Good," said Ruth. "Great. I'm relieved. But are you sure you don't want to do this? You can absolutely pursue it, if that's what you want. I will support whatever you want."

"We should have kids," said Morris.

"We should?" They'd never discussed this possibility before.

"We should have three or four kids," said Morris. "Maybe five or six. And I think I want to do something different with my life. There are other things I can do. If we sold our apartment and moved out of Manhattan, we'd have plenty of money. We'd be rich in Denver or Detroit. There are lots of things I'm good at. Maybe I could be a greenskeeper at a golf course. I like mowing grass. I like raking leaves."

"We are not leaving New York," she said. "What are you talking about? Where would we move? Fucking Detroit? What about our friends?"

"I don't care," he said. "Maybe we need to get past that."

"We need to get past having friends? What happened out there? How much did you drink tonight? What's next? Are you going to start going to church?"

Morris kept his eyes on the carpet. He noticed how dated it was. He could almost see the seventies. He'd never noticed that before. He stalled for time and tried to construct an explanation that would sound equitable to his wife. Instead, he just told the truth.

"My life has peaked," he said. "It's time to start a new life. Maybe there can be another peak."

Ruth tried to stop herself from rolling her eyes. She failed. Ruth was the kind of woman who always wished her husband talked about his feelings more than he did. Now it was actually happening, and she was surprised by how annoying it was. Why was this happening tonight? It had been a wonderful weekend, up until now. "Go to bed," she said. "I'm going back to the party. You go to sleep. Sleep it off."

"Can you please send Roger up here? I need to talk to Roger," said Morris. His own voice reminded him of a little boy. Ruth rolled her eyes again and tromped down the stairs, making sure her steps were loud enough to signal disgust. The bedroom door was wide open. Morris could hear voices murmuring from the living room, followed by muffled laughter. Soon after, he heard a large mammal bounding up the stairs, two steps at a time. Roger ducked his head to slip under the top of the bedroom doorframe and sat on top of an oak desk by the closet. They both wordlessly worried the desk might collapse, but it kept its integrity.

"Ruth says you're having a nervous breakdown," said Roger, smiling the way he smiled at his own jokes. "I hope she's right."

"Do you remember the first weekend we came out here?" asked Morris.

"Yes," said Roger. "Bush was president."

"Do you remember a conversation we had on the deck that weekend? It was super late, maybe two in the morning. There were a bunch of us. We found that VHS tape of *Working Girl* and watched it on a black-and-white TV in the basement? You were still dating that girl with the big feet? We didn't know the grill needed propane, so we just ate corn on the cob for three straight days? Do you remember any of that?"

"I remember all of those things, except for the conversation on the deck."

"It wasn't really a conversation. It was more like a lecture," said Morris. "You were out of your mind on mushrooms. You were lecturing everyone about the greatest hypothetical moment any person could potentially experience."

"That doesn't sound like me at all," said Roger. "Although I'm guessing I said it would have been if Michael Jackson had recorded a duet with Prince that was produced by Nile Rodgers."

"No, not that. Although I think that was maybe mentioned."

"Was it about eating a bucket of chicken on the summit of K2?"

"No, that was a different night. That was when you were listing all the things that money can't buy."

"Was it about riding on the back of a Kodiak bear through a forest fire?"

"No."

"Did it involve Thomas Pynchon skullfucking J. D. Salinger?"

"No."

"Was it about the possibility of seeing a whale struck by lightning?"

Morris confirmed the query with his eyes.

"Jesus fuck," said Roger. "There's no way that actually happened. Did that actually happen? Is that what you saw out there? Are there whales around here? Since when are whales something we can see from the dock? What did it look like?"

Morris stared at his shoes and held his hands above his head. "It looked like what it was."

"You know, people have done the math on this," said Roger. "You multiply the number of whales on earth with the percentage of time whales come to the surface against the odds of lightning striking the water. Something like that. Calculus is involved. I can't remember the exact answer. It's like four point eight or four point nine—five whales a year, basically. Five whales a year get struck by lightning. If you believe the math, which I don't."

Morris listened to Roger, his favorite friend. Six-foot-eight. Three hundred and forty pounds. Never played sports. Never been in a fight. Never depressed. Never exactly correct.

"I need to change everything," said Morris.

"I agree," said Roger. "There's no going back from this."

"I'm not joking."

"Neither am I."

Morris reclined onto his back, his legs still dangling over the bed's edge. The mattress was itchy and uncomfortable. It was like lying on a bale of straw. He'd slept on this bed at least three dozen times, but he'd never noticed this before. He'd never noticed it wasn't comfortable.

"Why do you think you said that?" Morris asked. "All those years ago. I mean, you were joking. I know you were joking. You say idiotic things all the time. But still. Why did you say the greatest thing that could happen to anyone was to see a whale get struck by lightning? Why would you possibly say that, of all possible things to say? What was your point?"

Roger offered no response. He didn't need to provide a point. His point had been made.

"I'm going downstairs," said Roger. "Do you want me to send Ruth back up here?"

"Yes," said Morris. "We need to get started."

If Something Is Free
the Product Is You

I THINK ABOUT THAT SCREWDRIVER EVERY DAY. I THINK ABOUT IT MORE than I think about my parents. Most of my dreams involve screwdrivers, or at least the dreams I can remember. Sometimes I walk into a hardware store and just stare at all the screwdrivers displayed on the wall. It's like looking at pornography, minus that moment of release when whatever you've been looking at explosively becomes absurd. There are lots of reasons screwdrivers are different from vaginas, but that's one nobody ever talks about.

To fully explicate my acquisition of the screwdriver would require more pages than *Anna Karenina*, so I will be brief: I owed Jerome a favor, which I will not describe or explain. But I will say this: It wasn't a conventional favor. It was the kind of favor where, had we lived in a different time in a different place, I would have been obligated to follow him around for the next twenty-five years, waiting for the opportunity to sacrifice my life at his behest. I'd have been his Chewbacca. They say everything is negotiable, but this was not a negotiable thing. This was an obligation that could not be declined.

Jerome had gone to extraordinary lengths to steal this screwdriver (bribes, subterfuge, a physical transaction he refused to discuss, and the temporary electromagnetic manipulation of the metal detector leading into the workroom). I don't know why he wanted it or why he was willing to take such risks. I'm sure he had his reasons. But once he had it, he had to hide it, at least for a week. I was the obvious candidate, for obvious reasons. They would search every cell in the facility the moment they realized the tool was missing, and someone with Jerome's reputation would have his room torn apart. All the hard guys would be scrutinized and probed and interrogated. But the exploration of my cell would be considerably less aggressive. The guards liked me. I didn't look like the other inmates and I didn't have the guts to fake it. Nobody perceived me as clever. I was weak. I was even too soft for the Nazis. Jerome slipped me the screwdriver before anyone knew it had vanished and explained how to stash it. There were predictable places and not-so-predictable places. The key was avoiding both. The key was not hiding it at all. It was psychologically terrifying, because I had to consciously place it where it would be easy to see if anyone actually looked, based on the assumption they'd look right through it. Which they did. The two guards halfheartedly searched through my locker and under my mattress, but they mostly made jokes about the way I organized my socks. They were gone in sixty seconds. The black rubber handle was visible the entire time, sitting in a ceramic mug on the sink next to the Lava. It was so easy I actually cried. Now all I had to do was wait a few days and smuggle the screwdriver back to Jerome, which we both knew would be complicated in the wake of the investigation. But then it became uncomplicated, because Jerome died. They told us it was suicide, which always means the opposite. I assume his motive for stealing the screwdriver had something to do with the motive behind his death. Certain things can never be explained. I prefer not knowing. But the upshot was that the screwdriver was now mine to keep, and I was the only one who knew this, because Jerome never told anything to anybody. This might also explain why he's dead.

I'm not a useful person, to me or anyone else. That may sound like self-deprecation. It's not. It's self-awareness. In school, I took home economics instead of shop. I claimed it was for the girls, but it was actually just the work. Whenever I tried to help my father in the garage, he would constantly call me worthless. I never learned how to change my own oil. I can't even assemble stuff from IKEA. To portray myself as some kind of grease monkey would be more disingenuous than any crime I allegedly committed. I don't know shit about shit. But even I could tell this screwdriver was sublime. It was a Husky-brand three-sixteenths flat-head with a five-inch shaft. I'll remember those specs on my deathbed. Considering where I was, its utility was limitless. You must remember, I was living amongst illiterate geniuses who regularly turned toothbrushes into scalpels. Possession of an actual nickel-plated screwdriver was like possessing ten pounds of enriched uranium. You could dig with it. You could kill with it. You could take things apart. You could scratch through drywall, into the electrical system. You could shatter glass. You could use it as a projectile. You could melt the handle and repurpose the plastic, and the melting process would also get you high. I was told it could be used to strike an arc for welding, although that required additional ingredients. If you somehow got into a vehicle, you could jam it into the ignition and turn the engine over at least once, assuming the vehicle was more than twenty years old. It could work as a radio antenna, if you knew your way around electronics. You could mix hooch with it like an oil worker, which is why vodka and orange juice is called what it's called. You could use it for torture. You could fuck with someone's teeth. You could use it for weird sex. It was everything it was intended to be, and it was also everything else. There was a time in my life, before all of this, when I kept $40,000 in cash, inside a leather briefcase, in the trunk of my Lexus. It may as well have been manure. All I ever did with it was show it to drunk sorority bimbos when I wanted to impress them, and even that only worked half the time. I had so much junk. I owned two Jet Skis. I originally had three, but I lost one in a card game. I had a double-neck electric guitar, even though I never learned how to play a single-neck acoustic guitar. I had pants that looked like normal pants, but were actually produced in North Korea. My penthouse apartment was bigger than a bowling alley. Yet that three-sixteenths flat-head screwdriver was worth more than all of that shit combined. You have to lose your entire life in order to understand how worthless most of life is. You have to lose it all, all at once. That's the only way to gauge the value of anything.

Here's my confession: I manipulated a fake world, only to be indicted by a realer world and exiled into the realest world possible. And yet: There are certain social conditions that apply to all three realms. There are qualities—human qualities, human weaknesses—that ignore levels of reality. The reason I ended up where I did is not detached from the explanation behind how I survived undamaged. My misdeed, or what is classified as my misdeed, was based on the illusion of potential: People would allow me to hold their money, and I would allow these people to believe that this holding process was generating even greater money, as long as they never tried to possess the money I was supposedly generating. I realize some see this as lying, or even stealing. But that discounts the nuance. I never wanted anyone to give me *all* of their money. I only wanted their extra money. The money they didn't need. Here's the thing: Some people don't realize they're rich. This tends to happen when someone is born poor and falls into wealth (and therefore never stops thinking like a poor person) or when someone is born mega-rich and only ends up regular-rich (and thereby concludes they've failed). All I did was provide these types of clients an opportunity to view themselves as successful. They all had more than enough money to live, but they couldn't enjoy that money unless they believed they were so grotesquely wealthy that whatever they spent didn't matter. My skill was allowing that belief to flourish. I helped rich people feel rich. The nuance was that I needed to convince these people that cashing in on that success would also *complete* their success, by which I meant it would abort their success. That if they somehow got what they thought they wanted, there would be nothing more to want, and that a life without desire was a form of living death. I was quite adept at this, if I do say so myself. People loved the way I imagined their future. There was always another mountain to scale. There was always something bigger or deeper or more delicious. It was a credible vocation and a net positive for most of my alleged "victims." I simply got careless. I'd explain what happened, but it doesn't really matter. Suffice it to say that the power of my creativity was stronger than the power of my memory. I got sloppy with the minutiae. If one story is enough, three stories are redundant. It doesn't matter how well those stories are told: Details create contradiction and adjectives become anchors. But that is neither here nor there. We all make mistakes.

The night after Jerome died, I came to two conclusions. The first was that I had an object of value. The second was that this object's value was dependent on its belonging to pretty much anyone who wasn't me. Like my dad always said—I'm worthless. I'm soft. My aptitude with a screwdriver would be the same as my aptitude with a double-neck guitar. I wasn't going to stab anyone and I wasn't going to escape. I certainly wasn't going to figure out how to weld. I was less competent than every single person around me. But I did possess *potential*, and my competency with potential is world-class. I possessed an object that could, potentially, change someone's life. What I needed to do was twofold. The first step was making sure everyone knew I held the potential they wanted. The second was making sure this potential was never, ever realized. Which, to my credit, is maybe the only thing I actually know how to do.

There was this kid everyone hated doing three to five years for "theft by deception," which really just meant he constantly filled up his car with gas and drove off without paying. His name was Marty. He was hated for being a sniveling gossip, but that only meant he was hated for being popular. I took a piece of typing paper and traced the outline of the screwdriver as precisely as possible, and then I rubbed the pencil lead over the Husky logo to transfer the stencil onto the bottom of the page. I gave the paper to Marty. That was all the proof required. Within forty-eight hours, the knowledge was universal. Everyone knew I had the screwdriver. So I buried it. I buried it, and then a week later, I dug it up and buried it again, in a different place. I did this every week for the next twenty-nine months. It was an illogical thing to do, as every excavation provided an opportunity for discovery. But I always needed to know exactly where it was, and I always needed to assure myself that it was still there, and I always wanted to feel like it hadn't been that long since the last time I touched it. The machinations of male insecurity are hard to explain. It was like being in a long-distance relationship with a beautiful woman I didn't deserve. I constantly needed to check in. I constantly had to convince myself that nothing had changed.

Memory is strange and useless. It can't be trusted, not even a little. I'm tempted to say that everything was wonderful from that point forward, which is how my mind wants me to remember it. But I know that can't be true. I was still where I was. But you know, part of my previous life really did return with that screwdriver. The person I assumed had been destroyed by the trial was still there, hiding inside my skin, ready to strut and haggle and run the offense. Almost immediately, anyone who'd talked to Marty wanted to talk to me. A few were subtle. Most were not. Some offered trade. Some offered protection. Some dabbled in intimidation. Some used a combination of all three. But in every case, their methodology was irrelevant. Every new proposition received the same two responses, regardless of what they proposed. My first response was some version of "Yes. Of course. I agree. If I'm going to deal with anyone, I'm going to deal with you. I will give you the thing that you want." Which was immediately followed by my second response, which was always the same: "But not yet."

You want to stab your enemy in the shower? Great move. Your enemy deserves it, and I'll help make it happen. *But not yet.* Don't attack a man who's waiting to be attacked. You'll only get one shot at this, so wait until he thinks you've surrendered. His ribs won't be any less defenseless in a month. You want to escape? You have an escape plan? Tell me the details. I'm impressed. I suspect your plan will succeed, and I have the tool you need to make it work. *But not yet.* This is the wrong time for an escape. You know that as well as I do. Spring is better than winter, so wait until it warms up. I'll still have what you need in April. You want it now? I want you to have it. You totally deserve it. *But not yet.* Not quite yet. Timing is everything, and this is not the time. You said so yourself. Remember? You just said that, right now. Don't panic. Why would I lie? You know I'm going to give you what you want. You need to be smart about this, in the same way you're smart about everything else. If you weren't smart, we wouldn't even be having this conversation. Don't give in to emotion. Don't let desire trump your intelligence. The one thing we have here is time. Time is on our side. But not yet.

Money is not everything. They tell you that when you're little, and you believe it. Then you get a little older and you don't believe it. And then you get older still, and experience makes you believe it again. So what they say is true. They're right. Money is not everything. But what they don't tell you is that everything is money. If what you have is what they want, what you have is money, as long as you never give it to them.

I'm out now, obviously. I made it out, and I'm a different person, although not different in the way I feared. It turns out I was right all along, about pretty much everything. I just wasn't ready to understand how right I was.

Never Look
at Your Phone

PUSHING A BOY ON A SWING IS FUN, FOR THE BOY. IT IS NOT, HOW-ever, an equitable transaction. The division of labor falls some-where below master/servant and above human/horse. But there are still benefits for the pusher, boring though they may be: It's not physically taxing, there's no hiding or seeking, and the pusher is allowed to stand in one place for an extended period while daydreaming about whatever he wants. It's a way to be engaged with someone you love, on his terms and to his liking, with palpable exhilaration as the zero-emission fuel. It's a way to be with someone and a way to be alone. For the nine hundredth time, Freddie retyped these thoughts into his brain as he pushed his son skyward and denied the existence of his phone. If he looked at his phone, he would see what time it was, and it would be earlier in the afternoon than he wanted it to be. Sunday afternoons in the sum-mer are 236 hours. Still, he knew this was the kind of captivity he needed to appreciate. He knew there'd eventually be a point when he would be old and decrepit, and his middle-aged son would be occupied by his own secret problems, and the decrepit old man would long for those infinite afternoons when the middle-aged son was still forty inches tall. Freddie reminded himself of this inevitability as often as he could, particularly in these stretches when daydreaming was still a viable option. The only way to appreciate the present is to pretend it's already the past. Emotions must live in the future. But then he heard a voice, and it ripped him back to Sunday afternoon.

"Excuse me," said the voice, although not politely. Freddie looked over his left shoulder and saw a woman in a beret, holding the hand of a girl who looked to be seven. "There's a man in the park. He's wearing orange, he's eating fruit, and he's talking to the children."

"Come again?" asked Freddie.

"There's a man in the park. Dressed in orange. Eating fruit. And he keeps talking to the children."

"Where is he?"

"Over by the basketball court," she said. "Sitting on a park bench."

"Oh. Okay," said Freddie, still mechanically shoving his son every 1.8 seconds. "Thanks for letting me know."

He turned his head away from the woman but could sense she was still standing where she was, six feet from his shoulder blade, radiating annoyance. She stood there a long time before sighing ostentatiously and skulking away. Freddie was not sure why this conversation had occurred. He glanced down at his shirt, just to make sure he wasn't wearing orange or carrying a banana. He involuntarily reached for his phone, but stopped himself. "Keep daydreaming," he thought. "Don't reenter the atmosphere." But then he heard another voice, coming from the same direction. This voice, however, was a voice he recognized.

"Freddie?"

He looked back over the same shoulder. "Oh, hey," he said. It was Michelle. Michelle was the mother of Caleb, a boy who went to the same preschool as his son. Freddie saw Michelle twice a day, five days a week. They said hello every morning and goodbye every night. They had similar complaints about the ergonomic construction of strollers and often bantered about the viscosity of vomit. He knew she'd had a cesarean section but did not know her last name.

"Where's Rachel?" she asked, and Freddie explained that his wife was hungover from book club and needed a nap. Freddie knew he was now supposed to ask a similar question about Rachel's husband, but he could not remember the husband's name. All he could recall was that the guy either graduated from Michigan State or owned a Michigan State baseball cap. He was relieved when Michelle continued talking.

"Can you do us all a favor?" asked Michelle, evidently speaking for an unnamed maternal collective. "There's a strange man in this park. He's wearing an orange jumpsuit. He's eating fruit and talking to the kids. Can you go over and deal with this? He's making everybody uncomfortable."

"What's he saying to the kids?"

"How should I know?" said Michelle. "I'm not the person talking to him. Nobody's talking *to him*. But he keeps talking to the kids. It doesn't seem normal. Something seems off."

"I guess I could," asked Freddie. "But why me? Who am I?"

"You're the only other man in the park," said Michelle.

Freddie looked around. Her assessment was accurate. All the mothers were looking at him with pained nervousness. It was a modern kind of awkward: Freddie never knew if he was supposed to believe that a woman could handle this situation as well as he could, or if he was supposed to recognize that this was the type of institutionally unfair scenario where being a woman was inherently terrifying. He also didn't like that his masculinity was viewed as a necessary component of the request, particularly since he had no data on the size of the fruit-eating stranger.

"What am I supposed to do? Do you want me to physically remove him from the park?" asked Freddie. "I'm not sure I can do that. Legally or otherwise."

"Just go see what his deal is," said Michelle. "Please? I'm sure he's probably harmless. But still. I can watch Luke."

Freddie walked around to the front of the swing and grabbed both chains with his hands, stopping it dead. He crouched like a catcher and looked his son in the face. "Hey, man," said Freddie. "I have to go talk to some guy who's eating fruit. But look—your good buddy Caleb is here. You stay here and play with Caleb. I'll be back in five minutes."

"What kind of fruit?" asked Luke.

"That's an excellent question," said Freddie. "Maybe mangoes."

"How many minutes are five?" asked Luke.

Freddie smiled as he stood up. Michelle mouthed the words *Thank you* and pointed toward the far end of the park, down a slope and closer to the monkey bars. Purely for purposes of identification, Freddie considered inquiring about the ethnicity of the perpetrator, but immediately reconsidered (mostly out of fear of appearing racist but also because it seemed unlikely that any one park would contain two people matching this already highly detailed description). His mind shuffled through various concerns in the following sequence as he walked away from his son:

- Should I be doing this?

- How is this my problem?

- Don't look at your phone.

- You know, my kid is awesome. Crazy how every minute I'm with him, I want to be somewhere else, but every minute I'm away, I immediately want to get back.

- Don't look at your phone.

- Aren't orange jumpsuits what people wear in prison?

- Do I live near a prison? Is it possible to live near a prison without knowing where it is?

- Luke definitely seems smarter than Caleb. More verbally advanced, for sure. He knows how to ask questions. That suggests critical thinking.

- If this pervert tries to fight me, I'm going to be so pissed at Michelle.

- I bet Michelle used to be a real Susan Glenn, though. You can tell by her bone structure. You can tell by her confidence.

- Don't look at your phone.

- Why didn't they install the monkey bars closer to the swings? That's some bad urban planning.

- Oh look. There he is. There's the guy.

He was not an escaped prisoner. That, at least, was obvious. He was possibly homeless, but probably not. He was unshaven and a bit slovenly, but not to the level of Aqualung. His orange clothes were clean. His hair was combed to the side. He had a duffel bag half-full of fruit and was chomping on a pear. Was he closer to thirty-five or closer to sixty-five? Freddie could not tell. The mothers had incrementally herded all the children away from his bench, so he looked like a lonely person who loved citrus, waiting for a bus without a road.

"Hey there," said Freddie as he approached. He tried to wave in a friendly manner, but the motion of his arm more closely resembled an attempt to draw the attention of a helicopter. The orange-clad fruit-eater looked back and said nothing.

"Hey, man," said Freddie. "How are you doing today? What's going on?"

"I don't know," said the man in orange.

"I get that," said Freddie. "But I have a little problem here, and I hope this doesn't come across the wrong way. I'm here with my kid, and a bunch of other people are here with their kids, and some of the other people are saying you've been talking to the kids, and they don't like that. I don't know why they don't like it, but they don't. So maybe don't talk to the kids so much. You seem like a friendly person, and I think maybe the first woman who complained might have her own issues. You know what I mean? I'm not completely sure what her deal is. But just be cool with the kids."

"This is a public park," said the man.

"Yeah, I know," said Freddie. "I get that. I get it."

This was not going well.

"I can't help it if little kids are in the same park that I am," said the man in orange.

"I know. But you're sitting alone in a park, which is a curious decision for this kind of park."

"What kind of park do you think this is?" asked the man, though his question wasn't really a question.

"It's a normal park," said Freddie. "But it's the not the kind of park where people without kids generally go to, just to hang out and eat fruit. I mean, look around. How many adults do you see here without kids?"

"How am I supposed to know who has kids and who doesn't have kids?"

"You don't need to know that in order to realize it's a strange thing to do."

"Are you employed by the park?"

"No, I don't work for the park," said Freddie. "Why are you making this difficult? I'm just politely asking you not to talk to any children you've never met before. The other parents are concerned."

"But you're not concerned," said the man as he wiped pear juice from his chin with the cuff of his shirt. "They're concerned, but not you. You've been coerced."

"You know, I wasn't concerned," said Freddie. "But now I kind of am. Now I think it's a little disturbing that some guy in an orange jumpsuit is sitting on a bench eating a huge bag of fruit, trying to talk to random children and not recognizing why that's a bad idea."

"How do you know they're not the ones talking to me?"

"What?"

"The kids," said the man in orange. "Maybe the kids are talking to me and I'm just talking back. How do you know it isn't the kids who are bothering me?"

"Listen," said Freddie. "I'm not going to debate you on this. Don't talk to the kids. Finish your produce and go home."

"I'm not going home," said the man. "I'm not doing anything wrong."

"Fine. Then eat your pears and keep sitting here," said Freddie. "Just don't talk to any goddamn kids." Freddie thought this was a strong closing statement, due to his casual use of profanity. He turned to walk away.

"Wait," said the orange man on the bench. "Can I ask you a question?"

Freddie turned and waited.

"What time is it?"

Freddie started reaching for his phone before stopping himself.

"None of your business," said Freddie, aware that his response made no sense.

He turned around and walked up the hill, back toward Luke. His hands were shaking. The quivering embarrassed him, even though there was no one around to notice. Why was he so upset? The confrontation had not been violent or intense. He'd never felt threatened. But he'd started an argument with a stranger and lost decisively. His rival had outflanked him on every point, even though Freddie's core contention was reasonable. Now he'd have to explain to all the mothers why the weirdo in the orange jumpsuit was still sitting on the bench, still chowing fruit. They'd ask him what was said, and Freddie would have to explain that he'd told the guy to leave and the man refused, proving Freddie's uselessness. They'd want to know exactly how the conversation unspooled, and Freddie would defensively concede that the weirdo had a constitutional right to sit in a public park, which would make it appear as if Freddie were taking the weirdo's side. There would be accusatory questions he could not answer. Maybe it would be better if he just grabbed Luke and went home. Maybe it would be better to just become the kind of person they'd all assume he obviously was.

He reached the top of the hill and looked toward the swings. They were empty, surrounded by chaos. Mothers were running in all directions, pointing and arguing. Everyone was either talking loudly or texting furiously. Freddie could hear a siren in the distance, gradually drawing closer. Children were sitting on the ground in groups of three or four, staring at their parents and saying nothing. After a moment of panic, he saw Luke's red hair beneath an oak tree and ran to him as fast as he could, picking him up in one swoop like a sack of potatoes.

"Lukey," he said. "What's happening?"

Luke's expression was calm and focused, the same way it looked when he watched *Peppa Pig*. He considered his father's question.

"Something happened to Caleb," said the boy, and Freddie was instantly ashamed by the depth of his own relief.

Reality Apathy

T HE TEXT WAS FROM SUSAN, EXCEPT THAT IT OBVIOUSLY WASN'T. It came from Susan's number and mirrored her syntax and referenced a conversation they'd exchanged a few weeks prior, but it also included the phrase "weird flex, fam," a phrase Susan sometimes employed but only as a means for making fun of people who used media aphorisms unironically. There was no possible way Susan would use such language earnestly while pleading for a temporary Venmo transfer. Still, the algorithm behind this text deserved kudos. It had managed to replicate Susan's distinctive misunderstanding of punctuation and her propensity for needing money at odd hours of the weekend. There was a depth of humanity to the spam that felt novel. Micah wasn't fooled, because he was impossible to fool. But he was impressed.

The machines were getting better at this.

They were always getting better. You had to respect that.

Had this happened three years ago, Micah would have told Susan to change all her passwords. Had it happened last summer, he might have told her to consider encryption. But there was no need for that nonsense now. It would only waste both of their time. A better alternative was to just stop communicating with Susan entirely, at least until the new phones arrived that fall. She wasn't the type of friend where private inter-action was necessary. She rarely had original thoughts, and on the rare occasions she did, she wouldn't waste them on interpersonal conversa-tion. She'd post them in public. Her value was always accessible.

Micah walked and scrolled and walked and scrolled, his neck craned forward at a 120-degree angle. He toggled through time and space, learning all of the things. Here was the president, speaking to a gaggle of reporters on the White House lawn, eloquently criticizing a new sin-gle by Quavo. Probably not real. Here was some audio of Joel Embiid claiming Trae Young was addicted to krokodil. Probably not real. Here was a story about China considering an invasion of India. Maybe true? Probably not true. Here was a drone image of people sunbathing topless at the McMurdo research station on the continent of Antarctica. Probably not real. Here was a link to a sex tape involving the archbishop. Probably not real. Here was someone reporting that Matt Damon was about to be arrested, including an embedded clip of Ben Affleck arguing for his innocence. That felt like a perhaps. Here was some footage of an alien mothership captured by a dashboard camera in Russia. Another perhaps.

Downtown was so annoying these days. What was with all the moose holograms? They were everywhere now. Micah couldn't even remember if they were supposed to be advertising or if they were supposed to be activism. He'd read, or maybe he'd heard on a podcast, that a certain per-centage of these moose holograms were not holograms. A seven-year-old child had been trampled on Hennepin Avenue. Or was it that the moose was real but the kid had been a hologram? Weren't they doing that now? Keebler would know. He wouldn't know if the event had actually hap-pened, but he'd know if people were saying that it did. He and Keebler were supposed to meet for hot turkey sandwiches at Keys at the Foshay "around noon," which meant one-thirty. Micah still had two hours to waste, so he sat at a bus stop outside the diner and looked through a few hundred baby pictures of himself before returning to the ecumenical scroll. Here was the secretary of state having what appeared to be a stroke. Probably not real. Here was a list of ten facts he supposedly didn't know about Harry Styles, except he knew nine of them and at least four were definitely false. Here was a slide show about illegal immigrants from Mexico being sold into slavery by legal immigrants from Norway. Probably not true. Here again was the secretary of state stroking out, although this time from a different camera angle and without audio. Here was Mark Cuban looking directly into the camera and explicitly advocating Maoism. Probably not real. Here were three high-resolution images of an elderly woman masturbating with an assault rifle inside a Baptist church. Probably not real. Here was an octopus. Probably not real. Here was a biracial woman he'd never seen before, live-streaming herself from a cave, talking about the relationship between global positioning systems and pancreatic cancer. That one was fifty-fifty.

The next time he looked up, it was ten minutes past two. He could see Keebler through the frosted glass of the Keys front door, sitting at a booth, rewatching *The Room* on his wristwatch. Micah hustled inside and apologized for being late. Keebler said it was cool and that he didn't even know what time it was.

"You see the bishop taking the dirt road this morning?"

"Naw," said Micah. "I didn't need to see that. How was it?"

"Smart," said Keebler. "Seamless. But the action starts too fast and goes on for too long. Overproduced."

"That's exactly what I thought about the Matt Damon thing," said Micah.

"You mean the stroke? That was fake. That was fake yesterday."

"The stroke wasn't Matt Damon," said Micah. "The stroke was the other guy."

"What other guy?"

"I can't remember," said Micah. "Something supposedly happened to somebody. It doesn't matter."

A waitress with a beehive hairdo drifted over to the table and took their orders. Keebler wanted to finish the last ten minutes of the movie, so Micah took filtered photographs of the various patrons throughout the restaurant. When he rechecked the image he'd taken of an elderly couple sitting by the window, he noticed the silhouette of a moose hologram in the distant background, reminding him of the inquiry he'd pondered three hours prior.

"I have a weird question," said Micah.

"GIF of Michael Jackson eating popcorn in the 'Thriller' video," said Keebler.

"The urban moose holograms. Some of those holograms are real moose, right? Like, two percent or something?"

"I don't think so," said Keebler. "Is that true?"

"I thought there was a report about a little kid who got trampled on Hennepin."

"I guess I did hear about that," said Keebler.

"Well, then the involved moose would have to be real," said Micah. "You can't get trampled by a hologram."

"Is it possible they're *all* real?"

"That can't be," said Micah. "I probably saw ten of them on my way over here. What would they be eating? Shouldn't there be moose shit all over the sidewalk? Wouldn't they constantly get hit by cars?"

"You can't really hit things with cars anymore," said Keebler. "You basically have to try on purpose, and it still doesn't work."

"Maybe you're right," said Micah. "I don't really keep up anymore. Maybe all the moose are real. But how come you only see them downtown? Shouldn't they be all over the suburbs?"

"That's a good point," said Keebler. "They're probably not real."

"The possibility of all those moose being moose never occurred to me until just now," said Micah. "Now I'm always going to wonder. Every time I see a moose, I'll wonder if I'm seeing a moose."

"Don't worry about it," said Keebler. "You can't worry about that stuff. It doesn't matter."

The waitress arrived with the food. It wasn't what they'd ordered, but they ate it anyway.

Reasonable
Apprehension

C OME IN. SIT. RELAX. YOU'RE THE ONLY APPOINTMENT I HAVE THIS
morning, so we have plenty of time. Can we get you anything?
Water? Coffee? Green tea?

"No, thank you."

Did Jada take all your information?

"She did."

Did she explain the billing process?

"She said this first meeting was gratis, and then it would be a
hundred twenty dollars per hour after that, assuming you agree to represent me."

Yes. That's totally correct. And every hour is broken down into quar-
ters, so if something only takes fifteen minutes it's only $30. Almost
nothing takes only fifteen minutes, of course, but sometimes something
will take an hour and two minutes and the client will wonder why she was
charged $150 instead of $120. From a billing perspective, two minutes
and fifteen minutes are the same. Do you get that? From a billing perspective, two seconds and fifteen minutes are the same. We always round
up. Does that make sense?

"I think I understand."

I'm sure you do. It's not complicated. It's industry standard. Now, over the phone, you said you'd been charged with assault. Is the charge *only* assault, or was it assault and battery? Did you make physical contact with the alleged victim, or did you only threaten the alleged victim with the possibility of violence? Please be honest with me. Don't hold anything back. I need to know everything, so that I know what not to ask.

"I made no physical contact with the person. I did not even threaten the person. But the person felt threatened."

How did they classify the threat?

"The person believed I was going to bite them."

Were they correct in that assumption? Were you going to bite them?

"That's the problem. I don't think so, but maybe."

Uh-huh. Okay. I'm going to presuppose that you were intoxicated at the time of the incident?

"No, not at all. I don't drink."

Oh. Sorry. In that case, I apologize for my conjecture. I should stop making assumptions and just let you explain what happened. Tell me what happened.

"Do you want the whole story, or just the end?"

Let's start with the end. Who accused you of the potential biting? Was it an acquaintance? A boyfriend or, you know, a girlfriend?

"It was a stranger. Someone on the street, just outside of a 7-Eleven."

A stranger, on the street, near a place of business.

"Yes."

What was your interaction with the individual? What was the nature of the dispute?

"There was no dispute. We just looked at each other, and then the individual started to back away, slowly, into an alley, and I followed her. I walked in her general direction, which she viewed as an attempted following. The alley she backed into was a dead end, and she must have felt cornered. She pulled out her phone and called the cops, who must have been just around the corner. They arrived immediately. Like, in seconds."

And you said nothing? There was no verbal exchange between you and the alleged victim?

"No exchange."

Remember, you need to be honest with me. I'm on your side, no matter what you tell me. So did you really not say *anything*? There was no exchange whatsoever?

"There was no exchange. No conversation. No argument."

In that case, let me rescind what I said earlier: This might only take fifteen minutes. Any credible judge will throw this out immediately. You can't just look at a random person and accuse them of trying to bite you. You don't have any priors, right? No previous record?

"This is the first time I've been arrested for anything. But it might be a little more complicated than you realize. The alleged victim was definitely spooked. She told the pigs I appeared dangerous, due to the way I'd exited the 7-Eleven. She said I looked agitated, and I was, a little."

Why were you agitated?

"The water bottles."

Pardon?

"In the refrigerated section of the 7-Eleven. All the bottles of water, along with all the soda and all the beer. I was disturbed by the water."

You need to elaborate on this. Maybe we should go back to the beginning, whatever that constitutes. We have all morning. My slate is empty. I'm all yours. Tell me everything. Why were you agitated by the water bottles?

"Okay. Okay. Okay. Let me try to simplify this: Have you ever gotten a flu shot?"

Of course.

"And what happens when you get a flu shot?"

I don't get the flu.

"Sure, but that's not how it is for everybody. I used to get a flu shot every October, but now I never do. Because whenever I get a flu shot, I essentially get the flu, or at least flu-like symptoms, for the next two or three days. As I'm sure you know, a flu vaccination is a small dose of what the flu is, and I end up experiencing a micro version of the illness I'm trying to avoid. My body is hyperresponsive to everything. That's why I quit drinking alcohol. I quit coffee, too. That's why I don't use cough syrup or stay in the sun or consume gluten."

Fair enough. No gluten, no sun, no flu shots. You're a sensitive person. That's no crime.

"But I'm also a licensed veterinarian. I passed my state board examinations last April."

Good for you. That's a real accomplishment. All those little skeletons to memorize—dogs, horses, beavers. Human doctors only have to memorize one. But you still need to help me out here. I'm not seeing how your veterinary career connects to the arrest.

"Like I said, I never get a flu vaccination. The flu inoculation gives me a slight case of the flu, so I risk it. I just drink orange juice and wash my hands. But as a veterinarian, certain inoculations aren't optional. Certain inoculations are required by the state. And it so happens that on the morning of my arrest, I'd received all my necessary shots. Which might explain why things played out as they did."

Are you saying that—

"I was a little rabid that day. Not much, but a little. I had a slight touch of rabies."

You had rabies.

Not in totality. Not completely. I had rabies-like symptoms. I had the twenty-four-hour rabies, from the inoculation. My limbs were a little tingly. My pupils were dilated, so everything looked fuzzy. No appetite at all— just looking at the hot dogs in the 7-Eleven made me want to puke. A little hydrophobia, which is why the water bottles freaked me out. And I was fatigued and a little aggressive."

You were aggressive.

"I mean, sure. Yes. That's what she would say. I'm sure that's what the woman told the pigs."

What else did she tell them?

"I'm not exactly sure what she told them, because I was in the back of the pig car when they were interviewing her. But I'm guessing she said I came barreling out of the 7-Eleven, a little too fast but also noticeably limping."

You were limping.

"Yes. I was experiencing some temporary paralysis in my right leg. Anyway, I see this woman, and she sees me. And as I noted, my pupils were like manhole covers. I probably looked like I was on that drug rich teenagers take for dancing."

Were you foaming at the mouth?

"There may have been some foaming. But mild. Very mild foaming. Less than a normal tooth brushing. But we were in public, so maybe the mere presence of foam pushed some buttons. I can't speak for what was in her head. I had a terrible headache. We locked eyes, and we both stood there, face-to-face, maybe ten feet apart, for five or ten seconds. And like I said, there was no interaction. But I could tell she was nervous, and she started retreating, back into that alley. And I technically followed her. But I wasn't up in her grill. I kept some distance. I wasn't within pouncing range."

Why did you follow her?

"I can't answer that question without conceding a degree of culpability. That's on me. I was compelled to follow her. My natural inclination is not to follow unknown women into alleys, but I felt like pursuit was my privilege. I felt like nothing could stop me from following her, and her fear bolstered my confidence."

I'm going to ask you this directly, because it needs to be asked: Did you *want* to bite her? Did the notion of biting her enter your mind?

"I don't see that question as relevant. Under any normal circumstance, I have no desire to bite other humans. But this situation was atypical. I was maybe five percent rabid, which is the social equivalent of ninety-five percent indignant. Have you ever had sex with someone you hate? It was a little like that. I did not want to bite this woman. I did not. Would I have done so, had the police never arrived? Perhaps. But that still isn't a reflection of what I *wanted* to do."

Let's stay away from that line of reasoning. That's not a point in our favor. It would be one thing if you couldn't remember the incident at all. That we could work with. But I'm not sure a jury would be receptive to an argument built on the prospect that you knew what you were doing, but you weren't doing what you wanted to do. The average juror tends to frown on debates over semiotics and intentionality. We need to focus on the rabies. We need to hit the rabies hard. And it still won't be a slam dunk. If we were in England, no problem. Legal history is different over there. You can kick a guy in the ribs if you have epilepsy. You can whack somebody in the head with a beer bottle if you're sleepwalking. The Brits love automatism and hate peanut butter. That's the essence of their culture. But here, it's the opposite. You will need to shoulder some of the blame.

"I don't want to overemphasize the rabies. It's not like I was Cujo.

I didn't need to be put down. I only had a touch of rabies. Just a touch. If we viewed frothing the same way we view sniffling, nobody would bat an eyelash. But I know how these things go. I know how the media works and how gossip travels. If we push the rabies angle, I end up being marginalized as the vet who got rabies on purpose. It will destroy my business. It will be all over Yelp. Nobody is going to take their dog to a vet if they think the vet might bite the dog."

I understand your position. I sympathize. Nobody wants to be famous for having rabies. But our strategies are limited. You voluntarily asked for the vaccination, so we can't claim you were injected against your will. You're also a licensed veterinarian, so we can't claim you didn't recognize the symptoms you were experiencing. There are traditionally three elements to any assault charge: intent, reasonable apprehension, and harm. You said yourself that you can't explain your intent, so that's off the table. Biting someone is obviously harmful, so that's a dead issue. The only element that remains pliable is the question over reasonable apprehension. If you actually want to fight this in court, reasonable apprehension is all we have.

"What does that mean, legally?"

Reasonable apprehension has to do with how the alleged victim perceives the event. Was it reasonable for this woman to think you were going to bite her? Was she justified in her belief that a person she'd never met was about to gnaw a chunk out of her shoulder? That's our only possible point of contention. So what made her assume she was in jeopardy?

"I think it was my eyes."

What about your eyes?

"Have you ever looked into the eyes of an animal that knows it's about to die? Most people have, once or twice: the old family cat, a deer on the highway that's been struck by a Subaru, whatever. Of course, as a vet, this is something you encounter all the time. You're constantly looking into the eyes of a creature that cannot speak, yet still communicates an undeniable awareness that it's about to cross over into something unknown and unwanted. It's a horrifying experience the animal cannot grasp, and you can see the intensity of that fear intertwined with the depth of their confusion. They know they're not merely sick or hurt. They know something profound is happening, something worse than anything they've previously encountered, something that transcends their inability to understand the passage of time or the biological limitations of corporeal existence. They are petrified by an abstract understanding of something they cannot specifically comprehend. Once you see this a few dozen times, it becomes something of a diagnostic shorthand. The pet owner wants you to help the animal, but that animal knows it cannot be helped. Its optical desperation cannot deny the truth. My livelihood is defined by the pupils of mammals who cannot speak. So when I stumbled out of that 7-Eleven and locked eyes with that unfamiliar woman, dialogue was not required. Her thoughts were unconcealed. She believed she was looking at a raw animal, and the transparency of her panic made me stronger. She looked into my eyes, and then she looked into my mouth. She stared at my teeth. Something primitive wilted inside her. Her fear was undercut by bewilderment, and she started to back away, and an illogical force churning within the fluid of my spine told me to follow, because that illogical force was now in control. As long as she could see my teeth and feel my eyes, she knew I was in control. My sickness was my power."

Okay, wonderful. We're going to plead no contest here. It should take about fifteen minutes.

Just Asking Questions

HE WASN'T TRYING TO BE A JACKASS. HE WAS TRYING TO MAKE conversation.

"That was a terrible summer," said the average man. He was the most average man possible. "I thought I had turned a corner, socially and professionally. I was so excited about the future. I was twenty-seven. I was finally making a little money. I'd purchased a house. But then everything collapsed at once. I lose my job, for a mistake that was not my fault. I drive home in the middle of the afternoon, unemployed, depressed, and humiliated. And what do I find when I get home? My wife is sleeping with my best friend. In my own house. She was having sex with my best friend, in my own bed, in the house I'd just bought and suddenly couldn't afford."

"Are you sure he was your best friend?" asked the jackass.

"In retrospect, obviously not," said the average man. "I obviously know that now."

"That's not what I mean," said the jackass. "Was he really your best friend *at the time*? On the day before you realized he was making love to your wife, would you have classified this person as your *best* friend? Or was he just a normal friend?"

The room grew colder.

"I don't understand the question," said the average man. "You want to know the *nature* of our friendship? He was my best friend until he fucked my wife, which significantly changed how I viewed our relationship. We did not spend a lot of time together subsequent to the fucking. We did not remain on the same bowling team. What are you getting at?"

"I'm not getting at anything," said the jackass. "I just think it's interesting how these types of stories always seem to involve a person's *best* friend. It's always, 'My best friend stole my wife,' or 'My best friend got me involved in a bad business deal,' or 'My best friend died on prom night.' I never hear anyone say, 'My third-best friend stole my wife,' or 'A longtime acquaintance stole my wife.' It's always *the very best friend* who's implicated. That seems odd to me. It strikes me as implausible."

"You think I'm lying about this," replied the average man. There was an edge to his voice.

"Oh, absolutely not," said the jackass. "I'm sure this happened. It may have happened exactly as you describe. But I do wonder if there's some psychological reason people inevitably want to connect the worst moment of their life with someone they're compelled to classify as their greatest friend. It's not like I would have any less sympathy for you if you'd merely claimed it was a *close* friend. It doesn't need to be your *best* friend in order for your sadness to matter."

"I'm not asking for your sympathy," said the average man. "I'm telling you about an incident that happened to me ten years ago, an incident that ruined my life. This is as hardcore as I get, about anything. Yet the only detail that concerns you is the potential inaccuracy of how I categorize the person who had sex with my spouse? Go to hell."

"Just hear me out," replied the jackass. "This is not a criticism. I'm simply noting that memory is a tricky thing. Like, let's say you were describing a dream you had last night. You would describe that dream and search for symbolism. You'd look for details that had symbolic value. That's the only reason we care about our dreams. Well, as time passes, our real lives become more and more dreamlike. Distant memories have much more in common with dreams than they have with documents or photographs or facts. The past morphs and refracts and contradicts itself, and we can't recall precisely what happened, even though the thing that happened specifically happened to us. We end up looking for symbolism within scenarios we only half remember, and it's obviously more symbolic to be betrayed by your *best* friend, as opposed to just a random friend."

"Are you suggesting I only half remember watching my naked wife straddle my best friend?"

"Not quite," said the jackass. "What I'm saying is that this person might have become your best friend *because* he slept with your wife, at least within your memory. A best friend is someone significant. This thing that happened to you—this horrific infidelity, committed on a day that was already traumatic—deserves to be classified as a transformative personal event. It changed you. Had this never happened, it's possible you'd still be with your wife, and this friend—what was his name again?"

"Ian."

"This friend, this Ian . . . you might barely remember him at all. He might fall into that very large category of friends who seemed important at the time, but were really just temporary placeholders within the ever-revolving door of your circle of influence. And I realize that's a mixed metaphor, but I think you know what I'm getting at. If he hadn't wrecked your marriage, it's possible he'd just be a guy you used to bowl with. Was he the best man at your wedding?"

"He was not," said the average man. "Thank God."

"There you go," said the jackass. "Now, *that* would been symbolic. That would have been some tragic irony, full stop. But he was not the best man at your wedding. He was just a man. Your wife cheated on you, but only with a man."

"And that's supposed to make me feel good? That's supposed to make me feel better?"

"Yes," said the jackass. "You were not betrayed by your best friend. You were merely betrayed by a person. And, of course, your wife."

Though they would stay in contact for years, the average man would never grow to like the jackass, or his insights, or the way he made conversation. Technically, they did become friends. They were always friends. But that's not the way he would be remembered.

To Live in the Hearts of Those We Leave Behind Is Not to Die, Except That It Actually Is

HE LOOKED THE WAY A MAN CAN ONLY LOOK WHEN HE'S REACHED the point of no possible rally. Asymmetrically emaciated. Brittle. Invisibly shattered. It seemed as though his bones were vibrating in place. The room smelled like antibiotics and vomit cleanser and cold McDonald's french fries. The lights were bright and the air was synthetic. All of it was terrible. But he could still talk, and he wanted to talk, and she wanted to listen.

His life had been remarkable. All lives are extraordinary in their own way, but his was extraordinary in the way strangers could easily understand. For almost five decades, he'd humbly occupied the dead center of American exceptionalism. Every major newspaper had his obit updated and polished, ready for circulation the moment he surrendered. His daughter had received numerous voicemails from all the major outlets, some for purposes of fact-checking and some for purposes less noble. She hadn't responded to any request. This time belonged to her, and to her alone. There was no one else to share it with. She sat by his bed, all day and much of the night, holding his quivering hand and listening to words only she would get to hear. Maybe she would write about this in her next novel. Maybe she would keep these thoughts to herself. The only thing she knew for certain was that this period of excruciating pain was a period she wanted to remember.

"Nona," he said on the third day of his torture. "I want to tell you something."

"Yes, Papa."

He coughed for almost a minute, eventually spitting a spheroid of caramel-colored mucus into a clear plastic cup.

"I'm sorry," he said. "I'm sorry you had to see that."

"Never apologize," said Nona. "Just tell me what you want to tell me."

"Nona," he began, "have you ever had ants in your house?"

"No, Papa," she said. "Not really."

"You're lucky," he said. "When I was a boy, we had ants everywhere, all summer long. The kitchen. The bathroom sink. You'd wake up in bed and there would be ants in your hair. There was nothing you could do. Ants are almost impossible to exterminate. Do you know why that is, Nona?"

"No. Tell me."

"Because you can't kill them straightaway," he said. "They're not like cockroaches, where you just spray 'em with poison and they die in front of you. For every ant you see, there are a thousand more hidden inside the walls. The queen lives in the walls. The scout ants come into the house, find the food, and bring it back to the queen and the rest of the colony. If you kill the ants you see in the kitchen, the queen recognizes their absence and goes berserk. She starts producing twice as many ants as before. So if you kill all the ants you see, you end up with more ants than you had in the beginning."

Nona listened and nodded. She tried to will herself into memorizing every sentence. It felt asinine to memorize something so banal, but she knew how this process worked. These moments were not normal moments. Someday, this might be all she remembered about the greatest man she'd ever known.

"You can scare the ants away with peppermint oil, which makes your house smell like a candy factory. But there's only one way to stop them for real," he continued. "You have to feed them poison that doesn't kill them. Not right away, at least. You have to give them poison they love, poison they consider delicious. Slow-acting poison they'll take back to the colony and share with the queen and all the ants you can't see. The scouts need to spread the disease, so that they all die over time, slowly. But even when it works, it's awful. Because like I said, the poison that kills them is a poison they love. Which means that when you first put the poison down, the ant population goes up. For three or four days, you have more ants than ever before. And you can't kill any of them, because you need to let them haul the poison back inside the walls. You have to let them overtake the house. You have to *watch them* overtake the house. God, I despise ants. I really do."

He coughed again, this time harder and dryer. She poured him a glass of room-temperature water. It was a struggle, but he managed to choke it down. It worked like a drug. For a moment, his entire body relaxed.

"I love your stories," said Nona.

"I know you do," he said. "You're so kind. I love you so much. You were a wonderful daughter who became a wonderful woman, and then a wonderful writer. Watching that transformation was the joy of my life. It was for your mother, too. But you know, that story about the ants . . . that's not really a story. And I think you know that."

"I think you're right," she said. "But I don't care. I just like hearing you talk."

"You actually should care," he said slowly. "You need to care. I'm trying to explain something."

"Then don't talk about ants," said Nona. "Just speak from your heart."

"Are you certain?" he asked.

"Yes," she said. "Of course I'm certain."

"9/11 was an inside job."

Nona smiled. She loved her wacky father. Even now, at the end of everything. He was so clever.

But why wasn't he smiling?

"I don't get it," she said.

"What do you mean," he replied. "Weren't you listening to the ant allegory?"

"I was listening," said Nona. "How was that possibly about 9/11?"

"Isn't it self-explanatory?"

"Not at all," said Nona. "Papa, do you even know what you're saying?"

"About the ants, or about 9/11?"

"This isn't funny."

"I know it isn't," he said. "That was a tough morning. I have regrets."

"You have regrets?"

"It wasn't my idea," he said. "There was that first attempt on the North Tower, in '93. That was real. That just happened the way it happened. But then we started talking, and somehow the talking became a plan, and then at some point around 1998 the plan stopped being theoretical, and then we installed W and—"

"Papa, don't say these things," she said. "This is not the time."

"It is the time," he said. "I'm sorry, but this is the time. This is the time to have this talk. I was hoping the anecdote about the ants would make it easier to understand."

"What would it possibly help me to understand," said Nona. "I don't even know who the ants are supposed to represent. Are the ants the terrorists or are the ants America?"

"Isn't it obvious?" the old man asked. "I'll be damned. I've been working on that metaphor for ten years. But now that I've finally said it out loud, I see the problem."

The door opened. A nurse stormed into the room and vaguely apologized for interrupting. She adjusted the old man's catheter and replaced the bag of sodium chloride hanging above his shoulder. The feeble father and his flustered daughter stared in opposite directions. The nurse asked if he needed anything for the pain. The old man said he was fine for the time being, but maybe when she came back in an hour.

"Do they have you on opioids?" Nona asked when the nurse finally disappeared. "Is that what this is about?"

"Yes and no," he said. "I am on opioids, yes. Percocet, and I think some sort of drip. But no, that is not what this is about. I need to tell you these things. I need you to know who I am, who I was. I've never killed anyone, but I allowed people to die."

"Yes, of course," said Nona. "Except that I don't believe what you're saying, so you don't need to tell me."

"We killed that singer," he said. "Didn't make any sense, then or now. He wasn't even that political. His politics were like a high school kid's politics. The stakes were so low. But we had this whole Manchurian candidate system set up from those World Vision refugee camps, and when Carter lost to Reagan everybody thought we should go back and give it a try, since we were still dealing with Khomeini and Ron was more open to that sort of thing. We all assumed it would never work. The nutjob from Hawaii was just a trial balloon. I was watching *Monday Night Football* when it was announced. What a kick in the head. I remember thinking that Cosell handled it better than I would have expected."

"Papa," said Nona. "Why even say that?"

"Because I love you," he said. "Because you love me."

"I don't need to know everything you've ever done in order to love you," she said. "You're my dad. That's enough. I don't need you to tell me we didn't go to the moon."

"We did go to the moon," he said. "But only twice. And the second time, none of those jokers made it back."

There was a gentle knock at the door, which meant it must be the doctor (the nurses never knocked). A tall black man in an oversized white coat entered the room. He spoke to his patient without emotion, asking pointed questions and expressing no reaction to the answers. The old man recognized the physician's accent and asked how long it had been since he'd left Nigeria. The doctor seemed annoyed by the query but said it had been just over twenty years. After briefly examining the patient's adenoids with his forefingers, the doctor turned to Nona and asked if they could speak privately in the hall. The old man said he understood completely and did not mind. He said he was not afraid of other people's secrets.

"Your father is an amazing person," the doctor said when they were both outside the door. "He is withstanding an astonishing level of pain."

"Are you sure about that?" asked Nona. "How much morphine are you giving him?"

"Some," said the doctor. "But less than I would normally prescribe, considering the circumstances. He declines what most patients demand."

"He's saying a lot of crazy shit in there," said Nona. "Something isn't right."

"Your parent is dying," said the doctor. "There is no other way for me to explain. He is dying, and more quickly than his behavior suggests.

So we must make some decisions. We must decide when to diminish the systems that are keeping him alive and when to amplify the systems that provide only comfort. There are no more avenues for recovery. I am sorry to tell you this, but I must tell you this."

"Oh, I get it, I get it," said Nona. "It's awful. I'm devastated. Of course I'm devastated. Of course. But again, about these painkillers—what are the side effects? Is there a possibility that my father's physical problems are impacting him mentally? It is possible he's suffering from dementia?"

"Dementia? I do not think he has signs of dementia," said the doctor. "I am generally impressed by his awareness. He has asked me about Nigeria on more than one occasion, so perhaps his memory is not as keen as it once was. But your father is an old man. He is sharp for an old man, in my estimation."

"That's what I always thought," said Nona. "But something is different today. He is not himself."

"It's difficult to die," said the doctor. "It's a difficult thing to explain to oneself, or to other people."

Through the thick composite of the door, they both heard the old man cough, then wheeze, and then cough again, for a very long time, almost like a record album that was skipping. Nona wondered if the doctor would rush back inside, but he did not.

"Take care of your father," he said before turning away. "We will talk again tonight."

Nona went back inside. Her father was grimacing, breathing through his nose. She poured him another glass of room-temperature water. Again, he struggled to force it down his throat. Again, it helped instantly, more than logic would dictate. He regained his composure and smiled at his little girl.

"I like that doctor," he said. "He seems competent."

"Yes," she said.

"Nona, I want to tell you something."

"Yes, Papa."

"Nona," he began, "have you ever had a raccoon trapped inside your garage?"

Tell Don't Show

YOU ARE NOT STARING OUT THE WINDOW OF THE BUS. YOU'RE LOOK-
ing out the window of the bus but you're not staring. You're
blinking the normal amount. Your eyes fix on one object and
then another. You're doing this because the window is made of glass, and
because glass is translucent. You're not sighing or chewing the inside of
your cheek. You're not closing your eyes for long periods of time, as if the
world were too beautiful (or too painful) to see. The world is the same as
it was yesterday. You can look right at it.

But you don't feel good.

You're not depressed. That would be melodramatic. That would be
medically incorrect. But you don't feel good, and it seems like you're constantly evaluating how good you don't feel. There's an emptiness to your
life you can't talk about, mostly because it would be insulting to people
with problems more significant than your own. You're well aware that
your life appears comfortable to others. You don't hate who you are or
what you've become. It's way more complicated than that. Once, there
were many things in life you wanted, and you were able to get most of
those things, operating from the supposition that fulfilling those desires
would allow you to feel the way you wanted to feel. But that didn't happen,

to a degree that now seems laughably predictable. Nothing changed. Nothing changed, so you convinced yourself not to want things, except for one specific thing that you can't stop yourself from wanting (and is now the only thing you want at all). This specific thing is just beyond your reach, and you can't fully understand why that is, and you wonder if your inability to achieve this goal is inherently connected to the single-minded persistence of your obsession. You also can't shake the recognition that this ongoing process of desire and acquisition has never worked before, and that there's no reason to believe this final achievement would be any different from all those other unspecific achievements that had no impact whatsoever. Your awareness of that inevitability makes you feel stupid. You've committed yourself to a difficult dream that is almost certainly hopeless, and that hopeless dream has become the center of your existence, further convoluted by the perpetual realization that such an existence is actually not that terrible (and that you should probably just get over yourself).

You step off the bus. Your face is just your face.

The concrete is hard and flat and composed of cement, water, gravel, and sand. You walk north at a brisk stride, directly into the wind. This means something. It means you don't want to be late and that the wind is from the north. You pass an old man dressed as a clown, talking to a young biracial woman who looks appalled. You pass a soldier in military fatigues looking at pornography on his cell phone. You pass an aging Gen Xer carrying a copy of the Good News Bible. You notice all of these individuals. They are metaphors for nothing. You feel a few random raindrops on your face, despite the sun in the sky. It's raining while the sun is shining. That happens sometimes. It's a meteorological phenomenon unrelated to your worldview, which is that humans are conditioned to forget the most important things they experience, in the same way that dreams dissolve from your memory within the same moment you try to explain them to other people. There's a reason you believe this, although you can't recall what it is. A car passes close to the curb, and through its airtight tinted windows you recognize the melody of a muffled song you haven't heard in ten years. But the song itself is actually twenty years older than that, and the car's driver is hearing it for the first time, just now.

You arrive at the building before the rain gets cinematic. The address is 667 Avenue of the Americas. It's a conventional office building with above-average amenities. It's a fine building. You take the glass elevator to the nineteenth floor and head toward suite 84. The suite has comfortable chairs, a logical floor plan, and excellent views of the city. Most (but not all) of your colleagues have already arrived. You're particularly happy to see that John Person was invited to the meeting, as he is your best friend at the company. Person likes to play video games and drink Old Fashioneds. He knows a lot about Civil War history and sometimes wears a bow tie. When he was fifteen, his father had an ill-fated affair with a stripper, and one night the scorned mistress tried to burn down the Person family home, trapping John in his upstairs bedroom and forcing him to jump from a two-story window. But John survived with only a broken ankle, and he got over it, and his parents divorced amicably, and when he told you this anecdote at the office Christmas party it almost seemed funny.

You are attending a meeting about a television campaign you've been working on for weeks. It promotes a brand of dog food. You suspect there's a problem with this campaign, and your suspicion is due to an email you received. The subject of the email was "RE: PROBLEM WITH DOG FOOD CAMPAIGN." The problem had been described in the email message and was now being pedantically restated at the start of the meeting, because this is how meetings work. Your supervisor spoke first.

"The problem," Sharon began, "is that we are not reflecting the actual value of the product. This is not traditional dog food. Dogs go apeshit for this slop. I've never seen anything like it. Whatever they did to this dog food is literally having sex with the taste buds of the dog. But our commercial literally doesn't reflect that."

"The dog in the commercial eats the food very fast," said Person. "It seems pretty transparent that he likes the food."

"No it doesn't," replied Sharon. "Dogs eat everything fast. Dogs eat their own puke like that. We need to show that the dog has a different relationship with this specific dog food. He can't just eat it like he's a hungry dog who wants dog food. That would be insane."

"What if we made the dogs talk?" said Grover Edison, a man famous for his predictable ideas. "What if one animated dog complains about how his food is only okay, and another animated dog unconvincingly argues that his food is marginally better, and a third dog bemoans how dog food just isn't what it used to be. But then the fourth animated dog—our dog—shoots a smug look toward the camera, and then he goes home to his dog wife and all his puppies, and they eat this great new dog food and frolic around in the yard and have this wonderful, edifying life. Our dog knows something the other dogs don't. But he's also not a jerk about it. He's relatable."

"That's terrible," said Sharon. "That's hack. That's how we sell *bad* dog food. That's like every other dog food commercial ever made. You're not grasping the paradigm shift: This dog food is actually *good*. It's not like the normal crap we push on the other dogs. This dog food has to scan as superior."

"So maybe we should just directly say that," says Person. "Maybe we should say that we've spent a lot of years making dog food commercials, and that most of them were different versions of the same lie. But this time, the dog food is different. This time, we're not lying. This time, the dog food truly is delicious."

"You know we can't do that," said Sharon. "It would look like a commercial."

"But that's the whole idea," said Person. "Why don't we just explain what the idea is?"

"Because people want to *see* the idea," said Sharon. "They want to construct the idea through the interpretation of unrelated actions. You know how this works. It only works one way: Don't show me the moon, show me a dog eating in the moonlight. That's what storytelling is. That's why we do what we do."

"But in this case, the only new idea is that this dog food is actually good," replied Person. "What kind of interpretive action represents the word *actually*? Won't people be more impressed if we just admit we used to be pretending, but now we're not pretending at all?"

"Yes and no," said Sharon. "That shift is what the consumer will extract from the story we construct. But we can't just tell them this directly. We need to show this nonfictional possibility in the same fictional way we show everything else. Except this time, the fiction needs to be true."

You listen to the argument, you consider what it means, and you fix the commercial. It's all you. You give the dog a problem and a desire, and the dog solves the problem to get what he wants. You bypass the logic and focus on the emotion, but the emotion is presented as logic and only falls apart if you refuse to embrace the emotion, which is an irrational way to respond to emotional logic. Your coworkers compliment your effort and concede that you are the best. When the work is finalized, they ask you to celebrate at the Irish pub directly across the street. You don't want to go, but you say yes, and you instantly regret saying yes to something you don't want to do. But it ends up being pretty fun, and you wonder why you always assume fun things will be awful. That night, two coworkers kiss for the first time. There's a minor shoving match behind the pool table. Einstein loses his wallet and his car keys. You go home, you fall asleep, and three months later you see the dog food commercial during a Knicks game. "Is this one of mine?" you wonder. You get up from the couch and pour yourself a bowl of cereal. On the way back to the living room, the ceramic bowl slips from your hands and shatters on the floor. It makes you think about terrorism, and about your love of cereal.

You are the only one who knows.

Slang of Ages

HOW MANY CLOWNS ARE STILL IN THE LOBBY?" ASKED DONNIE, well aware he'd become a caricature of gruffness. Walt looked down at his manifest and told him there were three. The first was a former history professor from a state college in the Midwest. The second was a woman who referred to herself as a sports sociologist. The third was a journalist who'd quit *The Times-Picayune* to attend law school, only to graduate and become a professional poker player. None of them seemed promising, but neither had the previous twenty-seven maniacs they'd interviewed throughout the afternoon.

"Let's do them all at once," said Donnie. "Let's get this over with. We have enough chairs. I never have any follow-ups, anyway." Walt agreed. He called the receptionist on the intercom and instructed her to send in the last three candidates as a group. They filed into the conference room with smiles on their faces and hands extended for shaking. Donnie and Walt did not reciprocate.

"Just sit down," said Walt, without looking up from the list. "Which of you is the college guy? The JFK guy?"

A bearded man in his late thirties sheepishly raised his hand.

"You're first," said Donnie. "You have two minutes. Go."

"Oh! Well, thanks," the red-haired man began. "As noted in my application, I was recently terminated by my employer, ostensibly for forwarding this theory online and proposing a three-hundred-level class around my research. Like a lot of my peers, I assumed academia would be a place where I could grapple with unconventional ideas. I was naive. So when I saw this opportunity advertised, I thought—finally. Here's a chance to follow my passion and galvanize my brand."

"We don't care," said Walt. "We don't give a shit about your passion, and your brand can rebrand itself with its own cock. Get to the point."

"Sorry, sorry," said the unemployed academic. "I'm not used to this kind of interview. This is all new to me, so I'll cut to the chase: John F. Kennedy was a complicated man, living in a complicated time. When we look at the world of 1963, what we see is—"

"This is not the chase," said Walt. "Whatever you're about to say is not the chase. We're all familiar with John fucking Kennedy. You want to cut to the chase? The operative word is *cut*."

"Sorry, sorry," the man said again. "I wasn't expecting it to be like this, but I can tell you're both busy, so I apologize. My concept, in basic terms, is that JFK was not assassinated. Not really. He knew what was going to happen. He knew the CIA was going to murder him. So that's part of it: The CIA *did* kill Kennedy. That's true. But that isn't the interesting part. The interesting part is that Kennedy knew he would be killed and still wanted it to happen. This was a depressed person with debilitating back pain. He had loved Marilyn Monroe and felt complicit in her death. He couldn't get over the Bay of Pigs and never recovered from the missile crisis. He'd had enough. He went to Dallas knowing he would be killed during that parade, and he went through with it anyway, waiting for the bullet. Wanting the bullet. Which is the basis for my supposition, which is that JFK was the progenitor of suicide by cop."

Donnie and Walt looked at the professor, then at each other, and then back at the professor. Donnie gave him a polite nod while Walt gestured toward the bookish woman seated in the center chair. She took the hint and launched into her monologue.

"Let me open with a question," she said with buoyancy. "In your professional opinion, would you say that contemporary college football cheerleaders are less attractive than college football cheerleaders from the past?"

Donnie and Walt did not speak or react, assuming the question had been rhetorical. When they realized she was not going to continue until her question was answered, Walt said, "Actually, no. That notion had never occurred to me. But for the sake of whatever you're about to say next— sure. Whatever. Yes. My answer to your question is a conditional yes."

"You're joking," she said, "yet it's not a joke. The difference I cite is real. I have research and surveys that prove this. From a conventional, traditional, patriarchal perspective, modern college football cheerleaders at all five of the so-called power conferences are less sexually desirable than their peers from the past, relative to the population at large. I realize one could argue that this is a positive evolution. I would argue that myself. On a base level, this whole discussion is oppressive. But that's a different argument. My research has to do with explaining how and why this evolution transpired, regardless of the evolution's merit. So let me pose another question: Why do you suspect cheerleaders are less attractive than they used to be?"

Again, Donnie and Walt sat immobile and silent. They would not fall for this twice.

"The answer," continued the woman, "is the Internet. In the pre-Internet era, what was the best possible opportunity for a nineteen-year-old woman in rural Tennessee who had been conditioned to view her humanity through the lens of the male gaze? When a sexist, male-dominated society tells a young woman that her value is solely a manifestation of her physical attractiveness, where does that young woman gravitate? In all likelihood, she gravitates toward scenarios where her attractiveness is most readily appreciated by the public. In 1974, that would equate to the sidelines of a football stadium in Knoxville, cheering and posing for three hours in front of a hundred and two thousand spectators. But the Internet has muted the potential reward offered by a physical space. The Internet is a more robust, more practical avenue. That same young woman now has unlimited bandwidth to express her sexual truth, in a context she can completely control. Every second of every day, over twenty-five thousand people are looking at amateur online pornography. It's monetized and socially acceptable. It would be illogical for a present-day person desiring sexual attention to choose a venue with the limited scope of a football stadium. This is why college football cheerleaders are becoming less attractive: That niche population is losing its strongest candidates to digital platforms."

Donnie raised his eyebrows and almost seemed to say, "Hmm." But then he just coughed and cleared his throat, much to the woman's chagrin. There was a fleeting pause, broken by Walt's pointing toward the handsome husky fellow in the third seat. Walt rotated his index finger in a circle and the chubby dreamboat nodded optimistically. Walt nodded back.

"My gambit is just an observation," said the third applicant. "My gambit is that people who compare sex and violence often get the complexity of that relationship backward."

"No shit," said Donnie. "People who talk about ideas always get them backward. If they understood what they were talking about they wouldn't need to tell other people. But go ahead. Give us your little example. You have two minutes."

"Something I've continually noticed," said the deep-voiced fellow, "is that progressive pundits often express outrage over the fact that a violent action movie will get a rating of PG-13, but a thoughtful film with a little sex and a little nudity will somehow get rated R. They see this as hypocritical, and they're always worried that violent content will desensitize children to actual violence. The point they inevitably make is that sex is a normal part of a healthy life, while violence is aberrant and detrimental. But that, to me, is exactly why it's worse for a kid to watch actors having sex than it is for kids to watch actors killing each other. An erotic movie will warp the way a young person views his or her own sex life. They will compare what they see in the movies with the real sexual experiences they'll eventually encounter as young adults, and that will warp their perception of how romance and sexuality is supposed to work and feel. But violence? Real violence is actually super rare. You guys ever read Steven Pinker? From a statistical perspective, worldwide violence is continually disappearing. The average kid will never experience a gunfight, even if he lives in Chicago. He'll never see a woman tortured or a man pushed through a wood-chipper. Children are being desensitized to violent experiences they'll never actually experience. And let's say they *do* end up encountering violence. Let's say they *do* end up in a war or in the middle of a mass shooting. Wouldn't being desensitized to that type of event almost be preferable? Why would anyone want full emotional engagement with something so traumatic? I believe fake sex is worse than fake violence. That's my gambit, for your consideration."

As per usual, Donnie and Walt remained mute. It was impossible to tell if they'd even listened. The applicants squirmed in their chairs, unsure if they were supposed to speak but fearful of what might happen if they tried. Five people sitting in silence makes for an excruciating fifteen seconds. But then Donnie and Walt tranquilized, and they both smiled, and they thanked all three candidates with a sincerity that seemed only marginally rehearsed. Everybody stood up and the three visitors exited the room. The door closed and the lock clicked. Donnie returned to his chair. Walt stood in front of the window and watched a homeless man urinating on the sidewalk.

"So a hard no on the first guy," said Walt. "Agree?"

"Totally," said Donnie. "That wouldn't even work as a podcast. Nobody cares about Kennedy. I'm sure kids under thirty consider him a sex predator."

"We could maybe use him as a guest," said Walt, "if a cop ever kills someone famous. But that ginger beard has to go, and all that apologizing was pathetic. It felt like we were listening to Alan Colmes or something."

"I enjoyed the woman a bit," said Donnie. "She has that If Maddow Were Coulter vibe, or maybe vice versa. And I like how she mentioned how she's done all this deep research, but then never actually cited any research whatsoever. That felt smart."

"True. But can we really build a broadcast persona around football cheerleaders who are supposedly unattractive? That's two weeks of content, max. I mean, I like how she blames the Internet, and I love how she keeps the focus on how these people look as opposed to what they do. The B-roll opportunities are epic. But it's limited. If her core theory was about women in general, sure. But *only* cheerleaders? I don't know. Outside of Tuscaloosa and Texas, what's the demo?"

"That's the upside of the last guy, I suppose," said Donnie. "Violence good, sex bad. That translates to everything. And I like how he knew when to stop talking without being told."

"But why did he keep saying the word *gambit?* Was he trying to remind us he's a professional gambler? That was annoying as fuck."

"Yeah, that annoyed me, too."

Walt moved away from the window, toward the wet bar. He put two ice cubes in a highball glass and immediately dumped them into the sink. Donnie stared at the ceiling. There was nothing on the ceiling to stare at.

"Thirty people," said Donnie. "Thirty people today, thirty people yesterday, thirty people tomorrow. All worthless. There has got to be an easier way to do this."

"There isn't," Walt replied. "If there was, that's what we'd be doing instead. But there isn't."

"Can't we just find the hottest person who's willing to say whatever we tell them?" asked Donnie. "That was a good system. That worked for a long time."

"Today's audiences see right through that," said Walt. "They need to believe that the host believes that the deranged message the host is expressing is a deranged message the host believes to be true. *Authenticity.* Every focus group tells us this. *Transparency.* All the numbers point to that. It's never about being perfect. We can't just throw an attractive person on TV and feed them bad ideas. That's not enough anymore."

"But why do the ideas need to be bad?" asked Donnie.

"Because our show is going to be different," said Walt. "We're not going left and we're not going right. We're going all the way, which means we have to start at the end."

Slow Pop

HE WAS CRISP. THAT WAS THE WORD HE USED TO DESCRIBE HIM-
self: *crisp.* "Back off. I'm a little crisp this morning." Nobody
knew what that was supposed to signify, but it seemed accurate.
We all agreed not to disagree. "Let's get crisp, fellas." Sure. Let's get crisp.
One night he played us the Steve Martin comedy album *A Wild and Crazy
Guy*, recorded in 1978. During the opening three minutes of the set, Martin notices a two-year-old child sitting in the audience and makes a few
jokes about performing for a baby. "That baby was me," he told us as the
disc rotated. "My parents took me to that show. That's how I got crisp."

[Wait. Allow me to start again.]

He was focused. He was the most focused person I ever met, and his
self-identification with that quality was unyielding. In 2011, the mayor of
New York tried to ban horse-drawn carriages from Central Park. It was
all over the news. Around that same time, he found a carriage driver who
(somewhat justifiably) feared his business was doomed, and he convinced
that driver to sell him the leather blinders that affix to the animal's head.
Paid him cash, on the spot, right there on Fifty-ninth Street. I think it cost
him eighty dollars. But it wasn't that he wanted a souvenir or a memento.
He actually wore them. Whenever he was working on something around

the apartment, he literally wore horse blinders. He altered the bridle and fashioned a foam forehead brace for maximum comfort. He'd answer the door wearing horse blinders. He'd go to the public library wearing horse blinders. He'd wear them on the subway. When he was especially interested in a movie or a play, he'd strap on the blinders inside the theater, right after we found our seats. We assumed he did this for attention. He insisted it was a psychological advantage. "The blinders help. I need to stay focused. Horses got it on lock. Horses are dope."

[Allow me to start again.]

He was obsessed with preparation. "I prefer to be prepared," he'd often remark, which is not an unusual thing to prefer or remark. But he took this to a crispier level. He once told me he'd prepared a ten-minute best man's speech for almost every unmarried male he had ever met, on the off chance he'd inadvertently perceived one of these relationships incorrectly. "What if somebody I view as a casual acquaintance considers me his closest friend? I need to be ready." I told him this scenario seemed unlikely, and that even if his fear was warranted and the event in question came to fruition, he would still have several weeks to come up with an original speech that is wholly acceptable to deliver extemporaneously. "What if the couple is eloping?" he asked in response. "What if the wedding is being televised or streamed live on Facebook? I'm not going to give an unrehearsed wedding speech about a man I barely know to a worldwide online audience." Again, I noted that this scenario was implausible and certainly not something to worry about. "But that's the thing," he replied. "I'm not worried. You would be worried. I'm prepared."

[Allow me to start one more time.]

I want to tell you about this guy. I don't know why, but I do. And let me be clear: This is not a story about a guy. This is not a story at all. It's just information about a guy you've never heard of, a guy you will never meet, a guy who left and never came back. But there was something about this guy, this person, this citizen, this bipedal humanoid projection. I'm still dealing with him, inside my mind. I'm still arguing with him, every morning and every night. He had a theory he called "slow pop." It applied to everything. It was a field theory. The thesis was that anything that happens quickly should be forced to happen slowly, as this alters the natural exchange of energy and amplifies the experience in unexpected ways. He first mentioned this in a conversation about the male orgasm, but he found a way to apply it to almost anything we happened to be debating—state politics, Grateful Dead bootlegs, the Bundesliga. We never understood what his theory vindicated or why he believed it, until the night he attempted to demonstrate by making microwave popcorn in a conventional oven. Forty minutes later, our apartment building burned to the ground. In a sense, I suppose he was right: That particular experience was amplified in an unexpected way.

[Let me start just one more time, and then I'll give up.]

There's this process people go through, sometimes in high school and sometimes in college and sometimes when they're thirty-nine and sometimes when they're told they have cancer. It's the process of asking oneself, "Why do I exist?" The question is grappled with for days or weeks or months, and the conclusion inevitably falls into one of two categories—either that there is no reason, or that some manufactured reason is insufficient but good enough. However, there's an ancillary question that's grappled with far less often: "Why do all the other people exist?" This question is harder.

You spend all this time convincing yourself that you're not the center of the universe and that reality isn't some movie where you're the main character. You stare at the ocean and remind yourself that the waves crashing against the shoreline have been crashing that way for two billion years, and this realization proves your existence is a minor detail within a trivial footnote inside a colossal book that can never be opened or closed. But then you walk off the beach and put on your socks and shoes, and you try to live like everyone else, and (without even trying) you're forced to reckon with the conclusion that every perspective is fixed and that the most myopic way to view life is the only way possible. There is no alternative to being who you are. You remain the nucleolus, against your will. But what are we to make of all the supplemental particles that buzz around our atomic structure? What is the purpose of a person who punctures the membrane of that nucleolus, displaces a few electrons, and then disappears forever?

A guy comes into your universe and tells you he's crisp. For whatever reason, you believe him. He wears horse blinders and burns your home to the ground. Somewhere between his interview with the police and the arrival of the insurance adjuster, he gets on an Amtrak and never comes back. You knew him for two years. You temporarily loved him. You knew his name, but it's a name many people have. He cannot be found. You knew everything about him, but nothing useful. Now he's a story, a story you tell, a story you tell where there is no plot, a story that is not actually a story. He was in your life. But you were not in his.

[ ]

TITLE: *Super Awesome Sports Dynasties* (Eli Weinroth, editor)
PUBLISHER: Steele & Simmons Young Adult Press (copyright 2048)
LANGUAGE: English
PAGES: 164
LEXILE MEASURE: 1085L

— 99 —

despite the injury. Auriemma retired due to health concerns in 2021 with a career-winning percentage of .878, a mark that continues to stand. To this day, the Lady Huskies' 111-game winning streak remains unchallenged.

Perhaps the only other college cage dynasty to rival Wooden's Bruins and Auriemma's Huskies involves the strange-but-true four-year run by the Massachusetts Institute of Technology Beavers from 2007 to 2010. Prior to their ascent, the Cambridge-based research university (commonly referred to as MIT) was perceived almost solely as a scholastic institution, competing in hoops as a lowly Division III program. But a controversial administrative decision in 2006 temporarily altered the school's view of competitive sports, and with it, the culture of NCAA basketball.

— 100 —

According to Charles Murray's 2021 book *MIT: A History*, upheaval in the MIT philosophy department in the wake of George W. Bush's presidential reelection led to the curious conclusion that academic excellence must be pursued across all avenues, including activities that were primarily physical. This sea change coincidentally corresponded with the NBA's adoption of its so-called one-and-done rule, ushering in an era where high school basketball players were forced to wait at least one year before entering the professional ranks. The timing prompted MIT to pursue a radical reinvention of its identity: They would compete for national titles in basketball by exclusively recruiting players whose only expressed intent was to immediately apply for the NBA draft the following year. In order to sustain the institution's academic reputation, these particular student-athletes were regularly described and promoted as "nontraditional prodigies" whose social, ethnic, and class-based experiences made traditional enrollment standards irrelevant. Virtually all Beaver players from this era pursued independent study programs in philosophy and epistemology that did not involve classroom participation. Undrafted players almost never returned to the school as sophomores.

Due to MIT's $11 billion endowment, the development of the program was unusually aggressive, launched with the rapid construction of Donald Thomas Scholz Arena, a state-of-the-art 17,000-seat venue with unprecedented acoustics. Previously "Engineers," MIT's moniker was officially changed to "Beavers" in a high-profile rebranding initiative, accompanied by an unsuccessful (and widely excoriated) campus genetics program designed to incubate and raise an 800-pound semiaquatic rodent. Assertive lobbying by alumni Kofi Annan, former Pennsylvania governor Tom Wolf, and actor James Woods allowed MIT to be immediately reclassified as a major independent on the Division I level. The university elected to hire no head coach and permitted the players to govern themselves, in concert with a team of unnamed consultants (three of which were rumored to be then NBA coach and future Texas senator Gregg Popovich, flamboyant identity-based filmmaker Spike Lee, and art critic Dave Hickey). How and why so much top-flight hoop talent elected to attend a school with no coach and no basketball tradition remains something of a mystery. "It was a self-perpetuating phenomenon," wrote Murray in his widely criticized history. "It appeared that many of the student-athletes were attracted to Tech's unwavering willingness to publicly insist that they were, in fact, autodidactic geniuses who coincidentally excelled at the game of basketball."

The Beavers perfected a freewheeling, pro-entropy style of play that alienated hoop traditionalists. In their first season as a D-I program, the squad went 39–0. Led by the freshman trio of Kevin Durant, Greg Oden, and Mike Conley, MIT defeated defending champion Florida in the national title game 88–69. The following season was virtually identical, as the Beavers again finished 39–0 behind the frosh efforts of Derrick Rose, Kevin Love, Michael Beasley, and O. J. Mayo. The third season (punctuated by Player of the Year Brandon Jennings and "regular student" Jimmy Bartolotta) brought home a third national trophy, though the Beavers lost twice during the regular season and failed in their quest to match UCLA's eighty-eight-game win streak. The Beaver empire ended

— 102 —

after the 2009–10 campaign, when an MIT roster populated by Derrick Favors, DeMarcus Cousins, Xavier Henry, and John Wall finished the campaign 38–1, downing Butler 112–77 on the season's final Monday.

The abrupt end of MIT's basketball reign (and its subsequent return to Division III) was spurred by a confluence of contentious media events. An exposé by *Sports Illustrated* published during the 2010 Final Four anonymously interviewed twenty-five former Beaver players, most of whom were actively playing professionally in the U.S. and Europe. According to the story, twenty-two of the interviewees could not properly define (and in some cases remember) the academic field they were alleged to have studied during their time at the university. Equally troubling was a public walkout by much of the school's faculty in response to the 2009 commencement speech, delivered by popular TV personality Dick Vitale. A third factor was the discovery that longtime metaphysics professor Monroe Wrathbone, broadly viewed as the intellectual engineer behind the original decision to classify basketball no differently than mathematics, was not of sound mind (and had, in fact, spent almost twenty years unsuccessfully attempting to lure former NBA superstar Moses Malone into a sex dungeon he'd constructed one level below the basement of his Tudor residence in suburban Boston).

Though sometimes dismissed as a compromised anomaly, the 153 wins registered during the Beavers' fleeting sovereignty represent the last true dynasty for men's collegiate basketball, as the NCAA itself would collapse and dissolve over the coming two decades. It also serves as proof that even failed experiments can sometimes generate positive results, most notably the breakthrough text *A Critique of Existential Memory*, published by Dr. Gregory Oden in 2030.

I Get It Now

'M ALMOST YOU. WE'RE ALMOST THE SAME. WHAT YOU BELIEVE RIGHT
now is what I believed before, when it seemed like the only reasonable
thing to believe: "This is happening." What other conclusion could be
drawn? How could it not be true? But I was wrong about that.

Accept what I am telling you now. I realize you won't. Your eyes are
already angry. You're squinting and you're not blinking enough. You're
shaking your head. But that's fine. That's part of it. If all this were easy to
accept, I would be way more worried. It would mean I was wrong again,
in a context too complicated to untangle.

Let's open with the annoying part: the French guy. Remember the
French guy? We were really into that guy, the French guy, in college, and
then again, briefly, after that movie. The French guy whose name I always
mispronounced, undermining whatever point I was trying to make.
Remember when he murdered his life? He wrote that dumb thing, that
thing about how the Gulf War didn't happen. This, as you may recall,
was published when the Gulf War was still happening. I think it was
literally titled "The Gulf War Did Not Take Place." Man, did we mock the
fuck out of that essay. We were like, "But it's on TV. Missiles are going down
fireplaces." The French guy became a joke to us, for twenty-five years, up

until the day he died. And even after he died, since it was so easy to make jokes about how his death didn't actually happen.

But here's the thing: I get it now. I finally get it. Not the way he described it, because he was never particularly good at describing things, even though that was his only job. Yet in a broader sense, in a broader framework, in a broader broadness—yes. I know what he was getting at. And it's not like how it was in the movie. Nobody is using humans for batteries. This is not the work of robots. This is not the work of someone else. We did this. You're doing it now, and I'm helping. I can see it in your dead shark eyes, and you can see it in mine.

Here, for the sake of oversimplification, is a metaphor: Imagine you're watching a football game. It doesn't matter if you don't like football. Imagine someone dragged you along. All that matters is that you're there. You're at the game and you have terrible seats. You're sitting in the top row of the upper deck, hundreds of feet from the action. Maybe the angle is bad. Maybe the view is partially obstructed by a beam. The tickets were junk. But you're there, so you're invested. You're engaged by default. You can see the microscopic players running pass patterns and covering punts upon the artificial grass. Some of them are getting concussed. Some of them are ripping up their knees and writhing in agony. Some are taunting their opponents. Some are fluid and beautiful. You glance at the scoreboard. Statistics are being accumulated and points are being scored. There's a jumbotron that's allegedly broadcasting a version of the same game you're watching live, and the multitudes of people around you are cheering and booing and guzzling Bud Light and arguing over the potential outcome. All of those things are happening. Yet there's one detail removed from the equation: There is no ball. The players are collectively pretending to throw and kick and carry a leather prolate spheroid that does not exist. It has not been there for years. Perhaps it was never there at all. It's been absent for so long that most of the players aren't even pretending. They believe that the ball must be there, just as you do. They need to operate as if this game is genuine, because it would be terrifying to believe otherwise.

This is the whole world now.

I'm not suggesting this is a dream. I'm not saying that the thing you're crying about is not something worth crying about. I'm not trying to make you feel better or worse. It's just that I finally understand. I understand that dumb thing about the Gulf War. It wasn't a war. It was the reproduction of a war. It was a TV show about a war, except they used real bullets and annihilated real houses. The French guy was simply the first lunatic who noticed. The only problem was that he didn't go far enough. He fixated on the semiotics of the semiotics. He talked himself out of it. He was right the first time, before he tried to explain what he meant. The war didn't happen, in the same way what's happening now only happens if you believe it. The president? He's the president, sure. I mean, I guess he is. He won and she lost, or whatever. But he's obviously acting. He's pretending to be a president who shouldn't be the president. Nobody actually acts like that. Nobody actually talks like that. He's just doing what the character is supposed to do. On a conscious level, he knows he's not real. On a subconscious level, we all know this, too. He had a lawyer named Ty Cobb. Come on. He had a communications director named Hope Hicks. It's not like this was some kind of brilliant subterfuge. The people who voted for him were acting how they thought disenfranchised citizens were supposed to vote. The resisters who hate him are resisting because they have been self-programmed to do so. They believe they're driven by some greater moral imperative, because that would make so much more sense. But certain constructed feelings need to be constructed. None of this would work if those manufactured emotions were not manufactured. It's Method acting. This is all Method acting, including your reaction right now, to this.

What else can I tell you, friendo? It's an unscripted play, to the benefit of no one. There's no conspiracy here. No lizard people. We're in this together. We're both involved. Or maybe it's that I'm involved and you're committed. Can I choose to be uninvolved? Can you choose to be uncommitted? Are those options available? I assume they are not. Maybe I'm only telling you this because that's what I'm designed to do, which means I failed before I even began. I can tell you don't believe me. In your mind, you've already walked away. But the French guy was right. We are the same illusion we see. The president is not the president. It's only happening on television. And I've been told that nobody watches television anymore, so maybe it's not happening at all.

The Power of
Other People

H E AWOKE AT DAWN, MADE COFFEE, AND WENT BACK TO BED. THE plan, as always, was to rise with the sun and get to work, but that felt a bit performative every time he actually tried to do so. He worked inside a windowless room. Sunlight was inessential. In the future, it might be nice to tell other people he diligently started working every day at the crack of dawn. It might provide the artifice of tenacity. But that future deception was the only practical upside, and he could always just claim he did, anyway. There was no record of his movements.

He awoke a second time, five minutes before nine. He sat in the quiet kitchen, drank the coffee he'd made two hours earlier, and ate three peanut butter cookies and a cold sausage. He wore yesterday's clothes, except for fresh socks and underwear. The house, which had once seemed to be the perfect size, was now colossal and cold. He pulled on his rain boots and exited through the back door, traversing down a short gravel path to a wooden shed partially obscured by trees and shrubbery. He wondered if any of his neighbors watched him as he walked, and if they ever wondered who he was and what he was doing, day after day after day, alone inside the shed.

He opened the door to the shed and closed it behind him, all in one motion. He flipped on the overhead light and activated the space heater. He turned on the radio and tried to find a station that didn't talk about the news and didn't play music that reminded him of anything he'd experienced in the past. That was getting more and more difficult, but never impossible. He spent a few minutes staring at the plywood boards he'd cut yesterday with the jigsaw. They'd seemed perfect when he was carving them up, but now they looked deficient. He couldn't recut them, of course. You can't cut the same wood twice. He could theoretically start again from scratch, but the end result would be identical. He was always embarrassed by his own craftsmanship. It made more sense to just stick with the imperfect boards and return his attention to the titanium skull and the aluminum spine, although that would require him to focus on the wiring, and that would consume the whole day. It might be more efficient to instead start mixing the chemicals. The PVC piping needed to be treated with the lubricant. Another option was to get back to molding the fiberglass around the battery—that was all detail work and would take hours, but he knew he was good at it, so at least it would be satisfying. Mounting the keyboard and the amplifiers would be easy. That could wait until the end. The larger issue would be with the proximity of the fan to the nitrous and the coal, and there was no easy solution to that dilemma. He was going to use coal no matter what, even if that made no sense to anyone else. He'd just have to incrementally fiddle with the speed of the fan until he didn't notice the problem. That was almost the same as solving it.

The thing didn't look right. It didn't look the way he imagined, and that became more and more apparent the longer he worked. He could picture other people thinking it was impressive, but they'd be reaching that conclusion for the wrong reason. He could just as easily picture people seeing it exactly the way it was supposed to be and still thinking it preposterous, and he wasn't sure if that reaction would be better or worse. The thing had no utility. That was a given, and that didn't bother him. He only wanted it to look the way it was supposed to look and to operate the way it was intended to operate, in accordance with his own personal standards. But even if he were able to achieve that, he would still need other people to recognize that those unspoken goals had been achieved. He needed strangers to know that whatever they perceived was intentional, and that he had preconceived that perception, and that he was the person who'd made it happen.

He mixed chemicals for over three hours. The lack of ventilation made him nauseous and woozy, so he decided to walk back to the house and drink some ice water. He'd almost reached the back door when he heard a voice call his name from what sounded like a long distance away, almost as if the source was screaming in pain from the bottom of a well. But when he turned around, the man calling his name was only ten steps away, smiling and holding a leaf blower.

"Jed," the man said again, kind of like a question. He wasn't yelling at all, as it turned out. "It's Jed. Right? Jed?"

"Yes," said Jed. "My name is Jed."

"It's me," said the man. "Larry. From over there." He pointed over his left shoulder with his right thumb, back toward a house that was even bigger than Jed's.

"Nice to meet you," said Jed.

"We've met before," said Larry. "A bunch of years ago, right when we moved in. You all came over to the house. We tried to roast that pig?"

"Oh yes," said Jed. "I guess I do remember that."

"I see you every day," said Larry. "They let me work remotely now, so I can see you from my den. I see you walk down to that little building in the morning and I see you walk back at lunch and then I see you walk back down again in the afternoon. I never see you walk back at night, though. You must work late as hell."

"I'm lazy," said Jed. "I always start later than I want, so I have to make up those hours at night. And sometimes I lose track of time. I'm a real space cadet."

"Don't mug yourself," said Larry. "I dig your dedication. Self-employed?"

"Self-employed. Unemployed. Retired. Whatever you want to call it."

"You told me what you did back at the pig roast, but I don't re-member."

"Phones," said Jed. "I did stuff with phones, when phones were the thing to do. But I got out of that a while ago. I cashed out."

"And now you work there," said Larry, jabbing his blower toward the shed.

"Yes," said Jed. "In a manner of speaking."

"How big is that shithouse? I'm guessing maybe twelve by sixteen? Sixteen by twenty?"

"It's sixteen by twenty-four."

"What exactly are you doing in there?"

Jed couldn't tell if this was an intrusive accusation or a friendly ques-tion, though he knew his intoxication from the chemical mixing was the reason he couldn't decode the difference. He tried to think up a response that would fit either scenario, but every possibility felt stilted and unnat-ural. He ended up saying nothing at all.

"Sorry," Larry said clumsily. "That's your business. Not my busi-ness."

"No," said Jed. "No, it's fine. It's just hard to explain. I'm a space cadet."

"Really, no worries," said Larry. "I don't need to know what you do in there."

"It's no big deal," said Jed. "I have no problem telling you. It just won't make much sense. If I were describing what I was building to a four-year-old, I'd probably say it was a robot or a dinosaur. If I were explaining it to a college kid, I'd say it was an art installation. If I were trying to sell it, I'd say it was a self-driven amphibious contraption, unless I was trying to sell it to the military, in which case I'd claim it was an urban combat weapon. But it's actually not any of those things. It's just something I want to build."

"Wow," said Larry. "A robot dinosaur. I'd always assumed you were just a carpenter."

"I wish," said Jed. "That would make more sense. But also, it's not a robot dinosaur. That's only how I said I'd explain it to a child."

"How big is it?"

"When fully assembled," said Jed, "about twenty-five feet long and twelve feet high."

"That's bigger than the shed, you know."

"I'm aware of that."

"Can I see it?"

"Maybe when it's done."

"What will it do?"

"That's not really the point."

"Sure. I get that. But even so," said Larry. "What will it do?"

"It will do lots of things, but that's not why I'm building it. If I wanted it to do one specific thing, I wouldn't need to spend my time building something that doesn't exist. I'd just go out and buy the preexisting thing that already does what I want."

"I understand what you're saying," said Larry. "I mean, not really. Seems kinda nuts, to be honest. But we're all a little nuts. You know what I mean?"

"No."

"Well, that's why you're the artist and I'm the pharmaceutical rep," said Larry. "I'll let you get back at it. I got leaves to blow. Just wanted to come over and say hi, now that I'm home all day. Don't be a stranger."

"Yeah, I'm not an artist," said Jed. "But thanks for coming over."

Larry turned and walked away. Jed reentered the massive kitchen in his massive home and could hear the leaf blower fire up as the back door swung shut. In a flash, he fantasized about rushing back outside, grabbing the blower out of Larry's hands, and using it to smash him across the face. But that impulse passed in a nanosecond, and he immediately felt shame for having felt such a feeling. He didn't know Larry and didn't remember the pig roast. He had already forgotten that Larry was named Larry. And yet he knew, with every granular fiber of his being, that this pharmaceutical salesman had been right about everything. His neighbor was a jerk, but a jerk who could see right through him. What he was building was indeed nuts, and therefore stupid. It had no purpose, and a machine with no purpose is less than the sum of its parts. A machine with no purpose detracts from the world. He'd ultimately have to destroy his shed in order to put it together, and it probably wouldn't even do what it was supposed to do, even though it wasn't supposed to do anything. People would think it was a robot dinosaur, except for the people who thought it was bad art. It was his own fault. He was lazy and he wasn't creative. He wasn't dedicated enough. He was a failure, and he was going to fail again.

No lunch today, he told himself. You don't deserve lunch. There wasn't much food in the house, anyway. He wandered into the living room and sat on the couch, staring at the empty space that used to be a television. There were pine needles all over the shag carpet. Jed tried to remember the last time he vacuumed. It must have been a year ago. Maybe two years. Did he still have a vacuum? Yes, in the basement. He stood up and started toward the stairs, only to give up before he got there. Spontaneous vacuuming would be a misuse of time. The chemicals were already mixed. If he wasted the afternoon cleaning the carpet, the fluids would grow viscous and he'd have to start over. There was no time for the house. He needed to get back to the shed. He needed to return to his failure. Fuck that troglodyte with the leaf blower. We'll see who's lazy. We'll see who cares the least.

ACKNOWLEDGMENTS

I'd like to thank the following people: Scott Moyers, Brant Rumble, Daniel Greenberg, Melissa Maerz, Mat Sletten, Mike and Chrissy Maerz, Jennifer Maerz, Bob Ethington, Eli Saslow, Michael Weinreb, Jon Dolan, Greg Milner, Ben Heller, Alex Pappademas, Sean Howe, Rex Sorgatz, Mia Council, everyone who works at Penguin, everyone who used to work at Blue Rider, Florence Klosterman, all of my brothers and sisters, all of my nieces and nephews, Silas Klosterman, Hope Klosterman, and anyone who ever caused me to have a weird thought.